Mark McGunegill

Copyright © 2014 Mark McGunegill
All rights reserved
First Edition

PAGE PUBLISHING, INC.
New York, NY

First originally published by Page Publishing, Inc. 2014

ISBN 978-1-62838-886-2 (pbk)
ISBN 978-1-62838-887-9 (digital)

Printed in the United States of America

CONTENTS

Chapter 1:   The Long Sleep 5
Chapter 2:   Ceti 2 9
Chapter 3:   The Fertile Valley 13
Chapter 4:   The Landing 16
Chapter 5:   A Distant Battle 21
Chapter 6:   First Contact 26
Chapter 7:   The Amakites 31
Chapter 8:   King Malcor 36
Chapter 9:   Exiled 44
Chapter 10: The Search 56
Chapter 11: The Harites 65
Chapter 12: Transformation 75
Chapter 13: The Great Crusade 81
Chapter 14: Pursuit 94
Chapter 15: Battle of the Gods 102
Chapter 16: The Turning Point 113
Chapter 17: A Fire in the Sky 119
Chapter 18: Gabriel's Diary 131

CHAPTER 1
THE LONG SLEEP

Obscure patterns of light began superimposing themselves over what had been a pleasant but unfulfilled dream. The dream seemed self-perpetuating as it explored and relived the good doctor's lifetime as well as dozens of alternate lives. There was, however, a strange restriction in the physical movements of the dream's first person. This became especially frustrating during the more amorous excursions.

But as hard reality forced its way through the senses, the reason became clear. Dr. Dunn realized that he was indeed physically restrained. It was a cold metal chamber with a glass lid and about the size of a coffin.

Warm blood began once again to surge through his body, and with it came clear vision and real physical sensations. In just a few seconds, all of the knowledge and experiences of his life resumed their place in the forefront of his mind. The long dream had vanished, all but forgotten.

"Dr. Dunn, it's time to wake up." A soft female voice inside the chamber broke the dead silence. It startled him at first until he realized that it was only the computer.

"You have arrived safely at the Tau Ceti star system," the voice continued.

"Tau Ceti s—" the doctor muttered. He was again momentarily confused. But in a few seconds, as the injected stimulant began to take effect, he remembered it all.

Tau Ceti, the first neighboring star found to have at least one habitable planet. It became the new age of discovery by the science community and eventually by many world leaders. When magnetic propulsion was perfected in 2079, the people of Earth saw a long, elusive quest suddenly within their grasp—to travel to the stars. The interstellar vessel *Odyssey* was assembled in space. It was completed and launched on its historic journey in the year 2095.

The glass cover rolled back.

"Please remain still until your body restraints completely retract." The soft voice once again filled the chamber.

The semicircular metal clamps that contained intravenous injection lines and various sensors suddenly separated in the middle and retracted from around the doctor's arms, legs, and neck. The voice continued.

"You are now ready to rejoin the other members of the *Odyssey* crew. You may experience dizziness and weakness. This condition will pass in four to six hours. Please remember to consume only liquid nutrients for the next twenty-four hours. Thank you, Dr. Dunn, and have a good voyage."

The chamber voice finally went silent as the doctor took his first feeble steps out.

Dr. James Dunn was thirty-five years old when he entered the chamber to begin his long journey. He was a renowned surgeon and pathologist from Kent, England, in the Northern European Federation.

The dormitory compartment was only large enough to contain the six stasis chambers, three against each bulkhead with a walkway in the middle. The embossed Vinylite walk felt strange on the doctor's bare feet. As he looked down, he could see himself clad only in short briefs. Then he heard the soft swish sounds of his companion's chambers opening up one by one.

The doctor immediately recognized the other crew members as they emerged from their chambers as scantily clad as himself.

Commander Robert Clarendon was the next to step out. At age thirty-six, he was considered very young to command what would become the greatest voyage of discovery since Columbus. But the young commander was a highly experienced military pilot and a natural leader. Clarendon came from Toronto of the North American League. He was known for his quick-calculating mind, his persuasive manner, and a ruddy, boyish face that made him look ten years younger than he was.

Gabriel Evans, the thirty-seven-year-old anthropologist, was also from the North American League, specifically the city of Seattle in the northwest part of the former United States. He was the tallest of the three men on the crew. The son of an Anglan father and an Afran mother, he had dark and ruggedly handsome features. Gabriel also seemed to recover from the effects of hibernation faster than the others.

"Where's the coffee?" His quip went unnoticed.

The next few minutes proved to be quite awkward for the men as the three female crew members emerged from their chambers.

Lea Moreno, aged thirty-two, was one of the most popular geologists and mineralogists in the South American League. From Buenos Aires, she was fluent in four languages. She did not seem to be aware of the others as she came glassy-eyed out of her chamber. She placed her hands on her lower back and leaned backwards to stretch. Lea was particularly well-endowed, and Gabriel, despite extensive social conditioning, found himself staring at her.

Sandra Hirata, the biologist, at age twenty-eight, was the youngest member of the crew. From Honolulu in the Pacific League, she held two doctor of science degrees, one in biology and the other in oceanography. Sandra came out of her chamber as if she had just climbed into it a few minutes ago rather than twenty-three years ago.

She soberly walked toward the three men, who just happened to be standing in front of the small closets containing their robes.

"Excuse me, gentlemen," she said with an unabashed smile.

She pulled out her robe and wrapped it around herself in a single graceful motion. The men also grabbed their robes and put them on. Clarendon took out Lea's robe and offered it to her.

Dr. Dunn noticed that the final member of the crew was peeking out of her chamber. Marie Chenault was the flight engineer from Paris in the Central European Federation. She was an expert in navigation, engine systems, and computers. Marie was a small-framed, mature woman with a healthy, athletic body. At age thirty-nine, she was the oldest member of the crew. Dunn remembered a budding relationship between himself and Marie. Hoping to continue where they left off, he took Marie's robe over to her, holding it open.

"How do you feel, Marie?" he asked warmly.

"Fine, Doctor, thank you," she answered in her soft and delightful French accent, but without the glimmer of remembrance he had hoped for.

The doctor was a bit chilled by her seeming indifference. But he decided to wait for the effects of the hibernation gases to completely wear off and to just let things take their natural course.

"Congratulations, everybody," the commander blurted out, half-startling everyone. "We are the first humans to reach a new star system."

"That is unless they built a faster ship and beat us to it while we were sleeping the last twenty-three years," Gabriel answered back half-joking. But he did bring up a paradox of ever-increasing technology, which was uncomfortable to consider.

"Not likely," the commander returned sharply. He did not appreciate Gabriel stealing his thunder.

Commander Clarendon ordered everyone to their cabins to get dressed. They would meet again in the galley to take special liquid nutrients, and then all would report to the bridge. Most of the crew were anxious to see the planet that was their destination.

The commander herded them out of the dormitory like schoolchildren. But none of the others seemed to notice or object. Billions of kilometers from home and with only each other to rely on, the all-consuming thought in each mind was excited curiosity about what might lie ahead.

CHAPTER 2
CETI 2

The small yellow star Tau Ceti was growing larger in the bow view screen. Nobody but an expert astronomer could visually tell it apart from Earth's own sun.

Clarendon and Chenault took up their positions at the pilot console. Gabriel and Dr. Dunn stood fast in the back of the control room, spellbound by the sight of the star rolling above and past the ship.

The *Odyssey* was at that time only travelling about one-tenth light speed and slowing. They would not see Ceti 1, for it was now on the opposite side of the star. But long-range probes have shown it to be an extremely hot, lifeless world of iron and zinc with no atmosphere.

The Tau Ceti system has only five known planets, but the outer three are so distant that they are presumed to be frozen, dead worlds. But the planet Ceti 2 has prompted great interest ever since it was discovered. With a slightly elliptical orbit averaging 140 million kilometers, it seemed a likely prospect for life. And when, upon further study, it was found to have an atmosphere of nitrogen and oxygen and surface water, the prospect of discovering life became irresistibly compelling.

Dr. Dunn and Gabriel Evans were still observing with great interest as Commander Clarendon and Marie Chenault were piloting them closer to Ceti 2. Sandra Hirata and Lea Moreno had slipped away to set up their own laboratories. Dunn thought it incomprehensible that the women did not stay to catch the first glimpse of a new world.

The *Odyssey* slowed its approach to the blue-green world considerably as it became visible on the view screen. Clarendon switched on the multiscanner, which can detect transmissions in any frequency of the radio spectrum. Apart from the natural characteristics of the planet itself, Earth astronomers had no indications of what kind of life, if any, could be found on Ceti 2. But the World Space Agency had tried to prepare the *Odyssey* crew for a wide range of eventualities. Tau Ceti is a star 11.9 light years from Earth. Even long-range space telescopes could only see the planet as a small speck around the star. But many educated assumptions were made based on the evidence gathered. The inhabitants of Ceti 2 could be anything from protozoa to a high civilization eons in advance of Earth.

Agency scientists and linguists had prepared a greeting signal that *Odyssey* was to transmit upon final approach to the planet. It was based on the algorithm of the Universal Translator. But after more than thirty minutes of hailing and monitoring, there was no response and no trace of any type of radio transmissions emanating from the planet.

No artificial satellites or spacecraft could be detected around the planet. As the *Odyssey* drew closer, not even low-power transmissions on the planet's surface could be picked up. The *Odyssey* made several long-range orbits of the planet at first. No artificial lights, such as from cities, were visible on the dark side. Gabriel had an anxious lump in his throat as he pondered the possibility that this whole voyage as well as a good portion of his life might prove fruitless.

Dr. Dunn's gaze at the view screen was momentarily distracted when Sandra Hirata came up next to him. Sandra and Lea had returned to the bridge.

"Beautiful, isn't it?" Dunn remarked.

"It is, and it's also rich with life!" Sandra responded.

"Just look at the bio monitors," she added as she pointed to the monitors on which the graph bars were jumping strongly for all categories of known life.

By that time the *Odyssey* was establishing an orbit of just three hundred kilometers altitude. The oceans, continents, major rivers, and polar regions were all clearly visible.

Ceti 2 was remarkably like Earth in many ways, the main distinction being that the oceans only covered about 40 percent of the surface, as opposed to Earth's 70 percent. But Sandra and Lea were already speculating that these might be freshwater seas. The polar ice caps were smaller than those of Earth, and no tropical rain forests on the scale of those on Earth could be found.

A disagreement arose between Clarendon and Chenault at the piloting console, which sometimes became loud enough for the others to hear. Clarendon wanted to digitally map every square meter of the surface from pole to pole before discussing possible landing sites. Marie, on the other hand, was instructing the computer to search for structures, settlements, or any form of organized intelligence. The commander's wishes, of course, won out, and Marie silently but dutifully complied. That methodical process would take several more hours to complete.

Meanwhile, as time passed, Lea, Sandra, and even the doctor had left the bridge. Gabriel's initial fascination with the planet was waning. But he stood fixed on the monitors, hoping that, as an anthropologist, he could still serve a useful function on the expedition. After more than an hour had passed, fatigue was catching up with him, so he finally decided to return to his cabin.

Just as the automatic door opened, an alarm sounded on one of the console monitors. Gabriel immediately stopped and went forward behind Clarendon and Chenault.

"There it is!" Marie blurted out.

"Enlarge and enhance," Clarendon ordered with restrained emotion.

The image on the computer monitor was telescoping in on the large square object in the fork between two converging rivers. Gabriel watched intently as the computer enhanced the image.

"What sort of structure do you suppose it is?" Marie asked Clarendon.

But before he could speculate an answer, Gabriel answered from behind with unwavering certainty.

"It's a walled city."

CHAPTER 3
THE FERTILE VALLEY

After many hours of analysis from orbit, the *Odyssey* crew discovered five such cities in the expansive valley. The largest of the cities was, of course, the first one sighted. It was situated between two tributaries that fed into a respectable size river that flowed through the valley floor. After leaving the green valley, the river continued southward through a rocky, arid region before reaching the gulf of the sea. The builders of the city could not have picked a better location for commerce and navigation.

The valley and the surrounding hills were lush with green grass, scattered trees, and assorted crops growing on cultivated parcels outside the city walls. Each city was surrounded by a number of small towns and villages that spread out into the countryside.

It was now obvious to all that Ceti 2 was inhabited by intelligent life, and the excitement and anticipation was on everybody's face. Gabriel's earlier concerns about his relevancy had vanished as his mind became flooded with thoughts and speculations.

Before long, a serious discussion developed concerning exactly where they should land the shuttle craft, who should make the first trip, and how they should approach the planet's inhabitants.

It was mutually agreed that the shuttle should not land within sight of any settlement. Marie scanned a canyon with rather steep walls on the back side of the range of hills that bordered the valley on the east. Approaching from the desert, they should be able to fly in under the ridgeline and set down in the canyon. Clarendon agreed.

Lea suggested that the crew draw lots to choose the landing party, but the commander had made the choices based on reasons that he did not share. The party was to include himself, Gabriel Evans, and Sandra Hirata.

Landing at the base of that canyon would require a steep climb up the hill and then a brisk eighteen-kilometer hike to the nearest settlement.

The valley was fertile enough to sustain the five cities and surrounding settlements. But a few kilometers behind the eastern hills lay thousands of square kilometers of barren desert. Even the river, as it flowed into the gulf about one hundred kilometers to the south, was surrounded by desert. The green valley became more arid and barren as the desert encroached in on it close to the sea.

Gabriel pondered why civilization seemed to emerge and prosper in one isolated area such as this. Other areas of the planet were found with abundant freshwater, forests, vegetation, and other resources that could sustain a culture. But Gabriel thought about Earth's early history. Civilization on Earth did not develop in isolated pockets in various places. Instead it sprang forth from the Mesopotamian Valley and spread out from there. To this day, there is no scientific consensus as to why this occurred. Perhaps by studying the civilizations on Ceti 2, he hoped to find the answer to this and many other important questions.

Gabriel and Sandra enjoyed throwing what-if scenarios back and forth to each other, arousing some heated discussions to stimulate thought. When the commander finally permitted the ship's cameras to zoom in on the larger city, they saw, to their amazement, buildings and structures, but from their angle of orbit, they could not detect the beings that inhabited them. Gabriel was visibly excited.

"Calm down now," Sandra said with a smile.

The other members of the crew were also fascinated but tried to act professional.

"It looks like rock formations and mineral compositions are not going to be the top priorities," Lea said with a slight concern about her own relevancy.

"Everyone's skills will be needed on this mission," Commander Clarendon said to reassure her.

Marie fixed the *Odyssey*'s orbit in its present position. The commander and Marie would man the bridge in shifts. The others were advised to return to their cabins. They could hardly sleep that night.

CHAPTER 4
THE LANDING

The shuttle staging area was frantic with activity. The whole crew was there helping to load supplies and checking inventory. The shuttle itself was docked onto the outer hull of the *Odyssey* with a retractable airtight gangway between them and air locks at each end. But the airtight hatches were wide open as crew members were going in and out of the shuttle.

Clarendon and Chenault were double-checking the shuttle computers to make sure that the topographic and other digital mapping had been downloaded completely. Navigation coordinates for the predetermined landing site were also locked in.

Meanwhile, Gabriel was moving toward the gangway carrying a small hard case with both hands as if it were a priceless gem or a volatile explosive. Sandra was coming out of the gangway and noticed Gabriel's preoccupation with the small case.

"Is that it?" she asked quietly.

"Yes, this is the latest prototype," Gabriel answered, looking down at the case.

"Let's have a look," she said with childlike curiosity.

Gabriel carefully opened the case to reveal a round, disc-shaped, metallic silver object about ten centimeters in diameter.

"The Universal Translator," she said as she admired the beauty and simplicity of the design.

"This should make my job a lot easier, if it works on this planet," Gabriel said.

"Assuming the beings on this planet even have a verbal language," Sandra chided.

"What do you mean?" asked Gabriel.

"We don't even know what these beings look like. They may not have a mouth or vocal cords. They may communicate with body movements or telepathy," she pressed to elicit a reaction.

Gabriel closed the case.

"Sandy, go back to your microscope," he said with a scowl.

Sandra smiled as she continued on her way.

After almost three hours of excited preparation, the mood on board the *Odyssey* became more somber as the commander, Evans, and Hirata emerged from their cabins dressed in survival jumpsuits and rugged terrain boots.

The ship's computers confirmed what the long-range probes had discovered years earlier. The atmosphere on Ceti 2 was breathable by humans. In fact, the gravity and surface temperatures were remarkably similar to those of Earth at comparable latitudes. The explorers would not be burdened by cumbersome survival equipment except for aluminum backpacks containing dried food, water, first aid, thermal blanket, compass, and communicators. In addition, the commander carried a set of military field glasses containing a high-resolution digital camera. He also carried a high-wattage laser handgun, which was the only weapon on the expedition. Gabriel was in charge of the Universal Translator.

The shuttle was officially known as the *TLV* for *Terrestrial Landing Vehicle*. But it was unofficially christened the *Archimedes*. It had to be a rugged and reliable craft, for it was the explorer's only lifeline. Since the *Odyssey* was assembled in space and was built only for travel in space, it was never designed to land on any planet.

Chenault, Dunn, and Moreno stood silently, watching their shipmates enter the air lock. They knew that their time to explore Ceti 2 would come. But in the back of their minds was still the disappointment of not taking those historic first steps. Chenault would be in command of the *Odyssey* while the commander was away.

The air-lock hatches closed. Clarendon manned the pilot seat. Sandra Hirata took the navigator's seat, although their landing site was already preselected and programmed into the computer. Gabriel buckled in on a forward passenger seat.

"The board is green. We are go for departure," Clarendon spoke through the intercom to the *Odyssey* control room.

"Roger, *Archimedes*. You are green and go for launch," Marie's voice came back over the intercom.

The gangway retracted from the shuttle exterior hatch. The hydrogen engines were ignited, giving off a low-pitch roar, and then the docking arms were released. The shuttle pulled away from the *Odyssey*, slowly at first. When it cleared the ship sufficiently, the main thrusters fired up. The *Archimedes* sped away from the *Odyssey* so fast that in just a few seconds the great interstellar ship was nothing more than a dot in space and then out of sight altogether.

Although the shuttle had the ability to make a direct descent, the preferred procedure was to glide down through the atmosphere in a large spiral formation to save fuel. As they cut through the upper atmosphere, the blackness of space turned into a deep blue sky.

Gabriel and Sandra began to develop a greater appreciation of the fertile valley and its cities as they flew over the vast and desolate eastern desert. No other cities or settlements could be seen in the desert region from their current altitude, which was, at that moment, six kilometers and descending. The small shuttle craft could not be seen from the ground at that height, at least not by human eyes. The objective was to land undetected if possible and to avoid any contact with the planet's inhabitants that would frighten them or put them in a defensive or hostile frame of mind.

The spiral descent slowed and straightened out considerably. At less than one kilometer altitude, they could clearly see the canyon into which they were about to land. The shuttle was also then clearly visible from the ground. Gabriel mused over the idea that although the canyon was a good place to hide a space shuttle, it might be an even better place for an ambush, should anyone be so inclined.

The final descent was straight and vertical. The shuttle gently came to rest on a relatively clear and level plot of ground on the canyon floor.

"This is *Archimedes*. We have touched down," the commander proudly called to the *Odyssey*.

"Congratulations," Chenault's reply came over the radio.

The commander shut down the engines, and an eerie silence came over the cabin. Then in a low and pondering tone, the commander compared their historic achievement to other great voyages of discovery such as Columbus in 1492, the first manned moon landing in 1969, and the first men and women to set foot on Mars in 2028. The crew savored the moment until Clarendon radioed in that he was about to open the air lock.

The crew gathered and strapped on their equipment, including Gabriel's Universal Translator and the commander's laser sidearm. One final atmospheric sampling was done before the outer hatch was to be opened. The atmospheric composition and pressure were well within normal range for human survival. The temperature was a warm but bearable thirty-five degrees Celsius or about ninety-four degrees Fahrenheit. And the airborne microbes were very similar to those on Earth. In fact, Sandra noted that several of the most virulent strains of bacteria and viruses were conspicuously absent from the atmosphere of Ceti 2.

Clarendon stood before the air lock hatch. Evans and Hirata stood right behind him. The inner hatch opened, and the party stepped into the small chamber. When the inner hatch closed, the outer hatch opened, and the clean, arid air filled their lungs. The commander stood on the edge of the platform about half a meter above the ground. He turned to his companions and recited a prepared speech.

"We have not come to claim this planet for any government or for any people of Earth. We have come as explorers and ambassadors of peace."

With that, Clarendon stepped down upon the firm ground of a new world.

As the crew stepped out away from the shuttle, they surveyed the canyon with its steep, rocky walls to find the easiest route out. The explorers were in top physical condition when they left Earth. However, the hibernation chambers did permit a small amount of cardiovascular and muscular atrophy in the body. So the climb to the lowest ridge at over two hundred meters in the warm sun of Tau Ceti would make it a taxing first day.

The commander found a natural trail that wound its way up the steep hillside. Clarendon took the lead. Hirata followed and then Evans as the three explorers hiked up the narrow trail single file. One item that was missing from their equipment inventory was some kind of brimmed hat or visor, which would have come in very useful for such an occasion. Although their jumpsuits came equipped with a chemical cooling system, sweat dripped from their faces as the hot sun and dry air required many rest stops and water breaks.

The path they walked was rugged and steep, and the trail was intermittent. On one occasion, Hirata accidentally made a misstep, kicking a large rock loose, which rolled past Evans before tumbling down the hillside. The incident caused both to lose their balance and almost fall off the trail. Clarendon stopped to help Hirata.

"Sorry about that," she said, looking back at Gabriel with a smirk.

Evans regained his footing by himself, and the three continued their climb with caution. When finally the ridge was clearly in sight, it was then only about thirty meters above them. The goal was to reach the summit and set up camp at least one hour before dark.

CHAPTER 5
A DISTANT BATTLE

That night on the summit was cool and pleasant. All slept well in their light insulated bags. The sun on Ceti 2 cast a purple and pink glow on the high clouds. It was a beautiful desert sunrise with a view of more than one hundred kilometers of unspoiled wilderness to the east and north.

As the crew consumed their morning nutrients and packed their equipment to descend the western slope, Gabriel looked back and noticed some movement on a distant mesa to the northeast. He asked Clarendon for the field glasses to get a better look. Fifty-power magnification with image stabilization revealed a large group of very human-looking Cetians gathered. Closer observation indicated that the people were all, or mostly all, men, and not just men but soldiers clad in battle gear and bearing primitive weapons.

Clarendon wanted to look through the glasses, but deferred to the anthropologist to make the first assessment. The commander did order Gabriel to start recording, and with a push of a button, Gabriel was making a high-resolution recording of everything he observed through the lens.

It was becoming clear to Gabriel that there were two distinct groups or even armies, and what he was witnessing was a battle. From his vantage point, it was difficult for him to determine whether this was the beginning, middle, or end of the battle since both forces seemed to be regrouping. Gabriel took silent satisfaction in the thought that Earth was not the only planet in the universe to know war.

Closer analysis revealed that one group was more numerous and well equipped than the other. The larger army's advantage was clear. Their weaponry included metal body armor and helmets. The front-line infantry carried short, straight swords of a metal that looked like bronze. The blades were about sixty centimeters in length. They also carried round metal-clad shields. Behind this line were soldiers holding metal spears of about two meters length. And behind that line were about twenty metal-clad chariots drawn by a team of animals that looked very much like the horses known on Earth. The driver was in body armor with a side holder containing about six spears. In the back was a row of archers who did not wear body armor, presumably to allow for quick maneuverability.

The opposing army, by contrast, had little or no metallic armor or helmets. They had no chariots or archers. They seemed to consist mostly of fast-moving infantry. Most of the soldiers carried a similar-style copper or bronze sword and shields that varied in size and shape. Strategically, they were at a disadvantage because they had been forced onto a mesa that had a shear drop only about one hundred meters behind their position. The lines of the larger army were straight and wide. The smaller army was dispersed throughout the field with about five meters distance in any direction between each soldier.

Greater magnification also revealed some physical differences between the opposing forces. In general, the smaller force had darker skin of a copper/brown hue and medium brown to blond hair. The men of the larger group generally had a lighter complexion with dark brown to jet-black hair.

The cause of the conflict was not immediately evident. It could have been racial animosities, religious differences, territorial disputes, or any number of reasons that have permeated Earth's own bloody history. Gabriel and his companions were watching intently, hoping that they would not ultimately have to witness a slaughter.

The Cetian soldiers stood poised to do battle. The question was, who was going to make the first move? The air was thick with tension, not only for the combatants but for the Earthly observers as well. Even the sky was growing dark and ominous over the very mesa where the two armies were facing off.

Then, with a hand signal from the commander of the larger army, the archers moved in unison, placing an arrow in their bows. They pulled back and aimed up at a high angle to shoot over their own troops at the enemy. The officer swung his arm down in a quick motion, and suddenly a volley of arrows flew into the air, arching down and falling toward the opposing army. Not a single arrow hit its intended target. Some bounced harmlessly off upraised shields. The others stuck in the ground.

The small army stood still until an older man, who may have been their commander, held up what appeared to be the hollowed-out horn of an animal. It hung from a long leather strap around his shoulders. When he raised the horn to his lips, he blew out two loud notes twice in succession. After that, what happened completely baffled the enemy army as well as the distant observers from Earth.

The small army suddenly sheathed their swords and dropped to their knees and then lay prostrate on the ground. Those that had shields placed them over their heads with the edge into the ground in front of them. The others simply lay down and folded their hands behind their heads as they lay motionless. When their leader saw that all of his men were lying down flat and still, he then took to the ground himself.

"What are you seeing?" Hirata asked.

"They look human," Gabriel answered without removing his eyes from the field glasses.

"That's incredible," Hirata remarked, almost in disbelief.

"What's going on?" she probed.

"Shhh, wait a minute, Sandy," he said sharply.

Gabriel was watching the scene in disbelief, wondering if this was some form of capitulation. More than two hundred soldiers were lying helpless before a more heavily armed enemy of superior strength. He feared that the answer would be shortly forthcoming.

The infantry of the opposing army started to advance with swords drawn. All indications suggested an impending massacre rather than surrender. As the soldiers advanced, they let out a yell and started to run toward their defenseless enemy. The infantry and the spearmen were within a few meters of their intended victims when suddenly the dark grey cloud that was behind them seemed to sweep down and forward with a blast of wind so powerful that it lifted the soldiers off their feet and sent them flying or tumbling across the field.

"What's happening?" Clarendon demanded.

"I don't exactly know. It's like a tornado touched down on the mesa," Gabriel answered with his eyes still glued to the field glasses.

Clarendon became anxious for more answers.

"I didn't see a funnel cloud. Are you recording?" he persisted.

"Yes, yes," Gabriel answered with some irritation.

The wind blew in a single direction and with such force and intensity that shields blew off soldiers' arms and, in a few instances, pulled arms off with them. The army, which a moment before was to be delivered an easy victory, was being rolled and tumbled over the backs of their enemies like tumbleweeds or dry leaves.

Gabriel was shocked to witness such a sudden and isolated storm inflict so much damage so quickly. The smaller army continued to lie facedown and motionless on the ground. Not one soldier even dared to lift up his head to see what was happening.

The cloud and blowing dust was so thick that only an occasional glimpse of a rolling, mangled body could be seen along with chaotic horses and chariots. The army and all their weaponry had been blown past their prone enemies and continued to travel across the mesa and over the high precipice on the west side. Shortly, hundreds of men with their horses and chariots were dashed on the rocks some two hundred meters below.

Then, as suddenly as it began, the great wind stopped, and the sky cleared. After the calm returned, the soldiers who were lying facedown on the ground began to poke their heads up out of the dirt and look around. Some began to rise to their feet. Their enemy was nowhere to be seen.

The Cetian commander rose up, lifting his arms. He shouted out a few words, which seemed to be directed more to the open sky than to his soldiers. But at once, his men knelt down on one knee and bowed their heads low as if in subjection to someone or something that was not clearly evident.

"I can't believe it," Gabriel gasped as he finally lowered the field glasses from his eyes.

"Give me those," Clarendon said as he grabbed the glasses from Gabriel and looked out toward the mesa.

Sandra took Gabriel aside.

"What did you see?" she quietly asked.

"Two armies, one destroyed in minutes, hundreds killed. It was almost like they could call down the wind to fight for them," Gabriel answered, still in disbelief.

"But that's impossible," Sandra replied.

"Yes, impossible," Gabriel muttered as he looked back toward the mesa.

CHAPTER 6
FIRST CONTACT

Commander Clarendon established communication with Marie Chenault back on the *Odyssey*. He did not go into great detail about what the landing party just witnessed. He was more concerned about the ship's sensors tracking the source of the bizarre and unpredictable weather anomaly. But after almost an hour of scanning the entire hemisphere, no meteorological cause could be found to explain hurricane-force winds that seemed to suddenly come from nowhere, hit a small isolated area, and then vanish just as suddenly. That question and many other mysteries of Ceti 2 remained open for exploration and research to solve.

The landing party marched boldly down the hillside into the fertile valley and in sight of the great walled city. Upon reaching level ground, they came near to what looked like a wheat field that was ready for harvest. They walked through the field on a narrow path. The explorers kept looking over the acres of grain to see if they could detect any people. But none could be seen. The wheat field came to an end as a barley field emerged. About one kilometer past this field was the river, which was to be their immediate destination.

The water of the river was a familiar blue-green. The width, depth, and current were such that only the strongest swimmer could cross it without a boat or ferry. A large stone bridge provided a crossing upstream over the eastern tributary. And a distant sailboat could be seen working its way upstream from the south. The landing party stopped at the sandy bank to rest and to admire the beauty of their surroundings.

Sandra removed a tester from her backpack and dipped it into the water. It proved to be relatively clean and free of any harmful contamination. As the explorers walked upstream along the riverbank, they noticed shallow irrigation trenches dug about every one hundred meters to water the many crops growing in the valley. Based on everything observed of the inhabitants of Ceti 2 to that point, it seemed that they were still at a low level of technology comparable to that of Earth three to four thousand years ago. But speculation aside, all agreed that no final evaluation could or should be made at that point.

After a short rest, the group started their trek upstream along the riverbank. Gabriel scanned the horizon for any Cetian that might be visible, knowing how important their first encounter would be. As they moved closer to the great city, the crops and trees thinned out to a more open, grassy but rocky plain. Strangely, nobody could be seen yet on the open plain going in or out of the city. The rocky hills to the east became closer to the river as they advanced when suddenly they became aware that they were being watched. Behind a large granite outcropping, four Cetian soldiers on horseback could be seen staring down on them from a nearby hill. The landing party stopped, still and silent.

Both groups remained motionless for a couple of minutes.

"Now what do we do?" Gabriel asked softly to the commander while keeping his eyes on the horsemen.

"Be calm. Show them we're not a threat," he answered confidently.

Finally the landing party resumed a cautious walk up the river trail. But suddenly, the four soldiers on horseback galloped down the hill to intercept them. They split up, two to block their forward advance and two to block any retreat. All in the landing party were very nervous, even though Clarendon wore a laser sidearm and Gabriel carried the unproven Universal Translator.

The four horsemen soon arrived to surround the landing party in a semicircle, backing them up against the river's edge. Their horses stopped only a few meters away. The soldiers were all holding swords at the ready. One soldier blurted out an angry question. Gabriel carefully activated the translator. The soldier repeated the question impatiently. Then a second later, the translator's speaker sounded in English.

"Who are you?"

When the sound came out of the silver disc, a look of astonishment came over the Cetian soldiers. Gabriel tried to hide his fear and responded.

"We have come in peace as ambassadors from a distant land." Again the soldiers were incredulous as Gabriel's words blurted out of the translator in Cetian with a two-second delay.

"What sorcery is this?" the soldier demanded of Gabriel.

But before Gabriel could respond, another soldier shouted out, "They are spies, Harite spies!"

A third soldier rode up to within striking distance and raised his sword up over Gabriel's head. Clarendon's reflexes proved quick and accurate as he drew his laser pistol and aimed it directly at the blade of the uplifted sword. Suddenly, a blinding flash of silver-white light forming a narrow straight line and lasting only a split second hit the middle of the blade and instantly softened the metal, causing the blade to fold over as if it were thin rubber.

The startled soldier looked at his bent-over sword and touched the blade. He yelled in pain, flinching back and dropping the sword after badly burning his hand.

"They command the lightning," the fourth soldier remarked.

The Cetian commander then put a question to Clarendon in a much more respectful tone.

"Are you gods?"

Clarendon carefully holstered his sidearm while looking to Gabriel for guidance. Gabriel switched off the translator for a moment.

"Claiming deity status has often proved dangerous, even fatal," Gabriel advised just before switching the translator back on. Clarendon looked at the Cetian and responded directly.

"No, we are not gods," Clarendon answered in a straightforward manner.

The soldiers looked at each other.

The commander then asked, "Have you been sent by the gods?"

Gabriel directs an ever-so-slight positive nod toward Clarendon. Clarendon gives a reluctant yes after a moment of hesitation. But with that, the four soldiers put away their swords, bowed their heads respectfully, and then rode away. The landing party released sighs of relief.

"Well, I'm glad to see you're a good shot," Gabriel remarked to Clarendon with a tone of gratitude.

"I'm not sure we did the right thing," Clarendon said.

"About what?" Sandra asked.

"I'm not sure we should have told them that we were sent by gods," Clarendon answered.

Gabriel responded, addressing both of them, "Look at it this way: We have the best of both worlds. We have the protection of the gods, but we're not expected to act like gods."

As Clarendon began to walk ahead, Sandra stopped him.

"Wait, are we still going into the city?" she asked.

Clarendon turned back to Sandra.

"That's what we came for," he said.

The three marched cautiously forward as they watched the four soldiers in the distance ride over the bridge and through the city gates.

Clarendon reported the incident to Marie Chenault on the *Odyssey*. He ordered her to adjust the orbit of the ship to directly over the city. With direct surveillance from space, the landing party might be made aware of possible threats.

With the great city only two kilometers away, the explorers found the main road by which visitors and local residents travel in and out of the city each day. On the road, several local inhabitants were coming and going. Some were on foot, others were riding or guiding beasts of burden attached to crude wagons or carts. Most of the natives were not disturbed by the oddly dressed strangers. Some of the looks received by the landing party ranged from friendly to incredulous. But the real test for their reception into Cetian culture would come when they entered the city.

CHAPTER 7
THE AMAKITES

As the crew moved through the colossal city gates, they marveled at the engineering incorporated in the construction of the great stone walls, given the natives apparent low level of technology. The walls were indeed built as a fortress, over ten meters thick and more than thirty meters high. The large granite blocks which formed the walls were installed with such skill and precision that almost no mortar was used. Gabriel estimated that it may have taken hundreds of workers decades to complete.

The Earth visitors were being carefully observed by watchmen on top of the wall as they passed through the open gates. But no alarm was sounded and nobody attempted to stop them. Observations made from inside the walls, revealed the structures of the city to be an amalgam of various architectural styles and materials, from large public buildings of polished stone, to residences, apartments and other buildings made of stone, brick, and wood.

The Cetian inhabitants moving about the streets wore mostly tunics and robes of simple cloth. They would stop in mid stride to gaze at the strangely dressed visitors from Earth. Several others would peer out at the strangers from openings in buildings. As the explorers moved deeper into the heart of the city, the curious Cetians grew in number. The natives had started to gather in groups to watch the strangers. Activity and movement in busy street markets would come to a sudden stop as the Earth explorers walked by. Gabriel became more excited with each step.

"It's amazing!" He blurted out.

"It's like we went back in time. This is like any city of the ancient world! They're humans. They're humans!" Gabriel said, unable to contain his excitement.

Then he turned to Sandra Hirata.

"What do you think, Sandy?" He asked.

"You may be right." Sandra replied cautiously.

"Although it is incredible that evolution on this planet so nearly parallels our own." She added.

From the crowd, a small boy, who appeared to be about five Earth years old, ran up to Gabriel and pointed up at him repeating some indiscernible childish phrase. Before Gabriel could interact with the child, his mother jumped out after him and pulled him back quickly.

It is uncertain what drew the boy's curiosity, but Gabriel speculated that it might have been his jumpsuit or his darker skin color or both. Every native that they saw in and around the city had a lighter skin tone with dark colored hair. The landing party was feeling more anxious as the crowd grew more curious. Human psychology has demonstrated that curiosity can sometimes lead to suspicion, and suspicion can lead to fear, and fear could easily turn a crowd into a mob.

Suddenly Marie's voice blurted out over Clarendon's communicator.

"Is everything all right, Commander?" she asked.

Many in the crowd were taken aback by the disembodied voice which seemed to come from nowhere.

"There is a large crowd gathered around your position. Please activate visual." Marie continued.

"Yes, we are aware." Clarendon responded feeling uneasy with Marie's call, he answered softly and quickly.

"They are just curious. There is no danger. I'll call back later. Clarendon out." The commander placed his communicator back into the pocket of his jumpsuit.

Following that exchange, the landing party received several long minutes of uncomfortable stares from the crowd until one richly dressed, older Cetian man came forward to break the tension.

"Welcome to Amakine, friends. Forgive me. May I ask what land has sent you to us?" The nobleman's statements came out in English by way of the Universal Translator.

"A distant land beyond the great sea, a land called Earth." Gabriel replied.

"Earth? I have not heard of such a land. Are you ambassadors?" The nobleman asked.

"Yes." Gabriel replied respectfully.

"And we wish to learn about your people and your way of life." He added.

The explorers learned from their interaction, that the natives of this region called themselves Amakites. But suddenly, the expression on the nobleman's face went from friendly and welcoming to somber and suspicious. Gabriel and the others perceived that something was wrong. Gabriel silently questioned himself as to what he could have done wrong. The natives were silent and looking at the landing party with contempt.

"What's wrong?" Sandra whispered.

Gabriel switched off the translator for a moment.

"It's me. I should have realized, societies at this level did not send out explorers just to learn about different cultures. They sent spies, usually as a prelude to conquest." Gabriel was frustrated by his diplomatic failure.

"What about trade, didn't the ancients send traders and merchants to distant lands?" Clarendon asked softly.

"Yes, they did. But what do we have to trade?" Gabriel responded.

"Maybe services or the ability to solve problems for them," Clarendon came back.

"We need to be careful. Our technology should not be used to supplant their natural development." Gabriel admonished.

Just then, Marie's voice came in over the communicator.

"Commander, there is a group of twelve to fifteen armed men approaching your position rapidly."

"Oh no," Sandra murmured.

"Let's just stay calm. We're here to interact with these people. We'll reason with them." The commander said without showing emotion.

Within a moment, a detachment of soldiers marched up to them and surrounded them. The soldiers were armed with swords and spears. But once they encircled the landing party, they did not act with hostility.

The commander of the detachment rode a horse and wore a decorated helmet and breastplate of brass. He looked resolutely at the Earth visitors and ordered them to follow. And so, without further question or comment, the landing party and their Amakite guards marched off toward a large, ornate building in the center of the city.

Back on the *Odyssey*, Marie Chenault, Lea Moreno and James Dunn were contemplating what their next move should be. On one hand, Marie needed to give them room to interact with the natives without interference. But if the landing party were to be taken inside the large compound, they could no longer be observed from space. She weighed the fact that although they all carried communicators and the commander carried a laser sidearm, there was a very real possibility that they could be easily and quickly overwhelmed by hostile natives. Still, she knew that there was not much she could do about it. Marie's decision was to wait for now until they received a call from the commander or one of the others.

Dr. Dunn was feeling a bit restless and offered to relieve Marie at the console. She thanked him but insisted on keeping her watch for at least the next few hours. If no contact was made with the landing party after several hours, Marie had the option of recalling the shuttle craft by remote control. She then would have the decision to continue to wait for the commander and the others to resurface or try to launch a search-and-rescue mission with just herself and the two remaining crew members.

The soldiers led the landing party through a great courtyard open in the center to the sky and surrounded by wide columns that supported wider covered corridors on three sides. The courtyard was a lavish garden of trees and floral bushes. A tile-paved walkway crossed in the center and went to the middle of each corridor. Four stone statues stood in the clearings of each corner of the garden. The statues were each about four meters in height and were images of Cetian deities. The bodies were humanlike, but they had the heads and appendages of animals and birds.

Gabriel and the others marveled at the beauty and mystery of their surroundings. The inhabitants of the city were obviously part of a polytheistic culture that had a high degree of sophistication in society structure, architecture, and artisanship.

They stopped within the great corridor and stood before two large wooden doors closed and secured with a massive slide bolt. The doors were ornately decorated with inlaid gold and silver and studded with precious gemstones around the perimeters. They were designed to be an impressive public entrance to the great palace, for they towered almost six meters in height and about two meters each in width. Two large silver rings on each door were used as a handhold for it took two strong men to push open each massive door. Four soldiers broke ranks to open the palace doors. As the doors slowly opened, the great interior was revealed as one of the wonders of their world.

CHAPTER 8
KING MALCOR

The main chamber was a large, ornate, and finely finished structure. The floor consisted of seamlessly laid large tiles of dark reddish-brown polished granite. On each side of the chamber were ten great columns of similar granite that towered from the floor to the massive ceiling more than ten meters above. Directly ahead was a large raised platform also tiled with polished stone. In the center of the platform was a massive throne seat carved out of black marble. On top of the back of the throne was a large image of the sun with flaring spires radiating around it and overlaid in pure gold.

Gabriel felt intimidated simply by the majesty of his surroundings, regardless of the armed escort lined up at attention behind them. The explorers did not have to wait long to see what would happen next. Two men wearing white tunics with red sashes emerged from anterooms on each side of the raised platform. They carried long horns of brass and stopped on the platform as they simultaneously faced forward. The two men placed the horns to their mouths in unison and blew out a loud but short triumphant call. Then they turned and retreated back to the antechambers.

A procession of twenty palace guards then emerged, which separated into two groups and took positions in front of the platform at each end. After the guards came, ten men in ornate robes moved in and stood next to the throne, five on each side. These were the advisors to the king and administrators of the various functions of government. Finally, a mature-looking man came forward on the platform. He held a solid brass pole about one and a half meters long with round balls on each end. The man stood next to the throne. This was the king's chief steward. He tapped twice on the floor with his pole and made a loud announcement. Immediately the Universal Translator began speaking. Gabriel quickly lowered the volume, but the translation was clear.

"Let all praise and honor our beloved king Malcor."

The Amakite king walked out to the platform in front of his throne as all heads bowed. He appeared to be a man in his thirties by Earthly comparison. He was handsome with well-defined features, light skin with dark hair, and piercing dark eyes. The king wore a simple black tunic with shiny silver trim. As the king sat upon his throne, the chief steward again tapped twice on the floor with his brass pole and looked directly at the visitors from Earth.

"Will the strangers step forward and present themselves to his majesty," the steward's summons came forth as all heads raised again.

The three glanced at each other in a desperate attempt to seek some sort of quick guidance as to what should be said to the king. But they also knew that it would be unseemly to be seen whispering among themselves. Clarendon stepped forward boldly with a diplomatic half-bow. He looked up at the king and began to speak.

"Your Majesty, we are ambassadors from a distant land who have come to you in peace and friendship. Our desire is to exchange knowledge between our people and yours."

When the Universal Translator came on to project the commander's words into Cetian, there were rumblings and startled looks on most of the faces in the court, even the king.

"By what magic does your medallion of silver speak?" the king asked.

"Not by magic, Your Majesty, but by the application of knowledge, the same way your builders can take raw stone and form it into this magnificent palace," Clarendon replied as he was beginning to feel more confident.

"You come to us strangely dressed. You come with weapons that can throw lightning at anything you point to. You come with a medallion that has the power to speak. Tell us, where is your kingdom and which gods do you serve?" the king continued his inquiry.

Clarendon had a quick mind, but it was, at that moment, racing faster than ever to come up with answers to the king's questions that would not get them killed or thrown into a prison.

"Your Majesty, our leaders have sent us a great distance to seek knowledge and to share knowledge with you and your people," Clarendon continued confidently.

"Our land is called Earth, and it is a long voyage by ship."

The king interrupted.

"You walked here from the Great Sea?"

"Yes, Your Majesty," Clarendon continued to weave his story in such a way as to be believable and acceptable to the king.

"Our land is far to the west. Our gods of knowledge and nature have given us the gifts that we carry with us."

After a pause for contemplation, the king spoke again.

"You are indeed fortunate to serve such powerful gods. Tell me, do you know of the Harite people?" The king's question seemed strange to them.

"No, Your Majesty," Clarendon replied, claiming true ignorance and not knowing where this was leading.

"Have either of your companions any knowledge of them?" The king's inquisition continued as he looked squarely at Gabriel.

"No, Your Majesty, we all arrived together to your country only yesterday," Clarendon responded as he was becoming a little nervous.

"I see. It is of no consequence," the king continued. "The Harites live in the eastern desert. They are thieves and murderers, and their intention is to steal our land and our country. We have been able to drive them back, and even now, a detachment of soldiers has been sent out to the desert to destroy a group of Harite raiders."

As the king spoke, the suppressed anger and hatred toward the Harites could be heard in his voice and seen in his eyes.

Clarendon, Evans, and Hirata glanced briefly at each other as they all were able to put the pieces together in their minds. The mesa battle that morning, the great wind, the dead soldiers were all part of the conflict that they had witnessed. That must have been the king's army and the opponents being the Harites of which he spoke. They wondered if the king knew what had happened. Had he received a report yet? Or could it come even as they stood before him? They realized why these people had such paranoia with strangers, for they had landed in a country that was in the middle of a war.

There was silence in the court for about one minute. Clarendon did not know how to respond to what the king just told him. Then suddenly the silence was broken by a soldier approaching the main doors from outside. The guards allowed him to enter the palace court. He moved quickly forward, holding a sealed scroll in his hand. He stopped about midway before the king and bowed low.

"Come," the king said as he motioned him forward.

The soldier stepped up onto the platform and handed the scroll to the king. He broke the wax seal and opened the scroll. As he read it, anger lit up his eyes, but he maintained his composure. He then lifted the scroll up in an upraised hand and called out.

"Shinak."

Immediately, his military advisor took the scroll from the king's hand and read it; all the while the king's gaze was straightforward. The king dismissed the courier without looking at him. He then turned his attention again to the three and spoke.

"We have just received word that some of our soldiers were killed in a sudden desert storm and that the Harite rebels have escaped—for now."

Then the king looked directly at Clarendon to interrogate him further.

"You say you wish to share knowledge with us?"

"Yes, Your Majesty," Clarendon replied.

"Would these include the powerful gifts that you have received from your gods?" the king probed.

Clarendon hesitated for a moment and then responded.

"We will share whatever knowledge we have that will be of benefit to your people."

"Commander!" Gabriel admonished with a whisper.

But the king and the court saw this and once again looked curiously at Gabriel.

"We are pleased to hear this," the king directed back to Clarendon.

"You see, the Harites are growing in number," the king continued.

"Although they live in tents, caves, and mud huts in the desert, they raid our towns and villages and desire to take over our whole country."

Clarendon and the others remained silent as the king went on about his enemies.

"They have no country or culture of their own, so they steal from others. I do not know how they survive. They acknowledge only one god who has no name or shape. They claim that this god directs every part of their lives from making war to telling them what they may or may not eat. But it is well known that no one god can rule over all things. They have been a menace to us for hundreds of years. Now tell us about yourselves. The three of you do not look like you are from the same country."

Clarendon's mind was racing to invent biographies for each of them that might be believable to the king and his counselors. He knew that the truth would be incomprehensible to these people, or worse, it may be taken by them as an attempt at deception.

Clarendon then went on to explain to the king that in the part of the world where they come from, different countries and people have come together to work for common goals. The commander gambled that travel for these people was limited to only a few hundred kilometers at the most and that he could convince them that such a unique civilization could exist somewhere in the far-off reaches of their own world.

The king looked puzzled at some of the commander's words but was intensely interested in all of it. Eventually, the king wanted more personal information about the three visitors.

"I perceive that you are an officer of some authority," the king probed.

"Yes, Your Majesty, but only over a small group," Clarendon answered.

"How many are you?" the king asked.

"Only six, Your Majesty, we three before you and three more back on the ship."

By that point, the commander's story was well developed in his mind, and he was going all in with it.

Then the king turned his attention to Sandra.

"Is this beautiful woman your wife?" he asked Clarendon.

"No, Your Majesty," Clarendon answered.

"Where is her husband?" the king continued. "Is this man her husband?" The king was referring to Gabriel.

Sandra was looking at Clarendon, awaiting his response with the same anticipation as the king.

"She is not married," Clarendon responded.

"Is she your slave?" the king asked.

"No, Your Majesty," Clarendon quickly retorted.

Then the commander's eyes lit up as he thought of an answer.

"She is a princess, the daughter of a powerful king."

Malcor seemed to accept that answer. He smiled and said, "She looks like a princess, and so she shall be treated as one."

The king then turned his attention to Gabriel.

"And who is this dark-skinned man beside you? He appears to have Harite blood in him, although I know this cannot be true."

Gabriel also turned to Clarendon in anticipation of learning his new identity.

"He is a priest of the god Namuh, who has given him the gifts of understanding the language and customs of many peoples." Clarendon went on, "The silver disc that he wears, which interprets languages for us, was built through knowledge given him by Namuh."

"I have not heard of this god. But that is a very useful gift," the king replied.

"We are pleased to have you here. You may stay with us here in the palace for as long as you wish."

The king was concluding his interview.

"My chief steward, Tabar, will see to your needs," the king ended with a somewhat forced smile.

"Thank you, Your Majesty," Clarendon responded with a respectful bow.

The chief steward, Tabar, then walked down the platform to escort the king's honored guests to their quarters.

After Tabar and the Earth visitors had exited the court, Malcor motioned to Shinak, his military advisor, to come near. Shinak approached the king and lowered his head so the king could speak to him privately.

"You will find out more about our guests. I want to know the secret power behind the objects they carry. I want to learn more about this far country that none of us have ever heard of. Do this secretly and enlist the aid of anyone you need, but they must also be discreet. Report only to me." The king's order was quietly spoken but firm.

"Yes, Your Majesty, it will be done," Shinak responded.

Tabar showed Clarendon and Gabriel adjoining rooms on the second floor where they were to be quartered. The rooms were luxurious by Cetian standards, but sparse and simple by modern Earth standards. A large balcony that overlooked the palace garden was at the back end of each room. The rooms each contained a bed with an ornately carved wood headboard, a large wooden chest for storage, a copper wash basin, and a brass bucket for convenience.

The men were about to ask Tabar about Sandra's quarters when they saw four young women approaching from down the corridor. Tabar informed the men that these were maidservants assigned to attend visiting royalty and other ladies of importance. Sandra was to stay in the royal chambers.

Sandra was feeling better about the idea of being a princess. Gabriel could not resist the temptation to tease her.

"Oh, Princess, if you get a chance between milk baths, don't forget to throw a bone to us peasants."

With that, Sandra smiled and walked off with her entourage.

Tabar bowed to his guests and excused himself, promising to return later to see to their needs. After Tabar left, Gabriel asked Clarendon a question.

"Commander, where did you come up with the god Namuh?"

"Easy," Clarendon answered, "it's *human* spelled backwards."

CHAPTER 9

EXILED

That night the commander made a detailed verbal report to Marie Chenault and the other crew members aboard the *Odyssey*. The Universal Translator records all of its input and output on an internal microprocessor. Gabriel uploaded all of the memory files directly to the ship's computer, which could actually produce a dictionary of the Amakite language.

    Gabriel did have a talent for learning extinct or primitive languages. He had, by that time, memorized several common Amakite words. Lea Moreno also shared that talent of mastering foreign languages even to a greater degree. Although her scientific training was in geology and mineralogy, she was fluent in four languages: English, Spanish, Portuguese, and German. Her duties aboard the *Odyssey* were light, which gave her an abundance of free time to pursue her own interests. Lea was restless to interact with the Amakites and to see their society up close. As soon as the ship's computer had completed a breakdown and translation of the Amakite language, Lea spent her free hours running tutorials and learning the language.

    Dr. Dunn found himself spending more and more time with Marie engaged in deep and personal conversations lasting hours. At one point, while pondering their future on Ceti 2, Marie confided with him that she did not believe that there was ever any real intention on the part of the World Space Agency that the crew would return to Earth. She based this on her analysis of the *Odyssey*'s propulsion system. There was not enough nuclear fuel left to attain the acceleration needed to make the return trip in two hundred years, much less the twenty-three years it took to get to this world. Also, the ship carried supplies and life support to sustain the crew for only about one year. And finally, there was the makeup of the crew itself, three men and three women, all top mental and physical specimens capable of starting a human colony on a new world. These things were never discussed openly by the agency or the crew, but these eventualities had to be in the minds of all but the most naïve.

The next morning, Tabar went to the quarters of Clarendon and Evans to invite them to a banquet starting at midday that the king was preparing in their honor. Of course, Sandra, as a visiting royal guest, was also expected to attend. Clarendon agreed without hesitation, speaking for all three of them. Tabar informed them that these affairs often lasted late into the night. He further assured them that their property would be safe in the room because the king would post an armed guard just outside in the corridor to prevent anyone from entering while they were away. Since it would not be considered proper etiquette to bring weapons, backpacks, and equipment to a party, Clarendon placed his trust in Tabar.

The banquet was a sumptuous affair that was set in a large assembly hall near the back of the palace grounds. About two hundred people were in attendance, including the king and his court along with various nobles and their families from the city. The food was laid out on a large center table. The enormous amount of food consisted of two different kinds of roasted animals. These were surrounded by cooked vegetables, fresh fruits, bread, cheeses, sweet delicacies made with honey and, of course, large vats of wine.

At the back of the hall was a great table at which the king, along with fourteen other high-ranking officials, sat facing the hall. Clarendon, Evans, and Hirata were also seated at this table as the king's guests of honor. Two servants were assigned to attend to this table continuously. All of the other guests could help themselves to food and drink and talked and mingled as they pleased. Clarendon sat closest to the king, and at that point, he was the one wearing the Universal Translator around his neck. That shiny silver disk, which could pass for a piece of jewelry, was the only piece of equipment that the crew carried with them.

Clarendon and Hirata were enjoying their status as honored diplomats. Sandra was given an elegant gown, fit for a princess, to replace her jumpsuit. They were both talking comfortably and quickly making good impressions with very influential Amakites. Gabriel was more subdued. He did, however, seek to engage people in short dialogue, mostly in an attempt to enlarge his understanding of the Amakite language and culture. Even in the midst of all the pleasantries, Gabriel was uncomfortably aware of the suspicious glares occasionally directed his way.

By late afternoon, the feast was in full swing, and the wine was flowing abundantly. The king, the landing party and most of the king's advisors at the table showed restraint in their indulgence, but some in the hall were getting very much into the festive spirit. Palace guards stood by to eject anyone who became too unruly. Shinak was the least talkative of the king's advisors at the table. After eating only a moderate amount of food and having no wine, he rose and asked to be excused, complaining of stomach problems. The king gave him leave to go, and he departed by the back door while holding his stomach and looking distressed all the way out.

A few minutes later, Shinak walked up to the door of the connected rooms where Clarendon and Evans were quartered. The guard in the corridor saw him but kept his glance straightforward as Shinak slyly stepped into the room. After closing the door gently behind him, Shinak scanned the commander's room. He noticed nothing unusual lying around in plain sight. Then he went over to the large wooden chest that sat against the wall between the door that adjoined the two rooms and the balcony. Shinak slowly opened the heavy lid and at first saw a linen sheet covering something. When he moved the sheet away, he saw the commander's aluminum backpack. Intrigued by the strange metal, which he had never seen before, he attempted to open it. The confines of the chest made it difficult to open while stored inside, so he boldly picked it up and set it down on the floor.

He noticed three latches across the dividing seam of the backpack. After pulling, pushing, pressing, and attempting to turn them, he finally, quite accidentally, put a finger under the clasp lever, and the latch popped open. He repeated this with the other two and then slowly opened the pack. Most of what the Amakite saw was a mystery to him, but two items he recognized.

The first item was the commander's communicator, which he had seen all three of the visitors carry identical ones on their belts. The second item that Shinak recognized was the commander's laser pistol. He carefully lifted the pistol out of its holder and examined it. He then stood up without taking his eyes off the fascinating object.

His curious mind was racing when he decided to test it out. The bucket next to the bed was moved to the middle of the floor. Then, while holding the pistol with both hands, he stood solidly, pointing it at the bucket, waiting for something to happen. After a few seconds, he started thrusting it and shaking it, but with no results. Then Shinak began issuing commands to the weapon.

"Lightning!" he shouted. Then he tried "Fire!" And then finally he shouted, "Namuh, make fire!"

Shinak was getting frustrated at his lack of results. He examined the weapon again, even looking straight into the barrel, which, in this case, was tipped by a synthetic crystal. Shinak pushed and pulled everything on the pistol, including the trigger. Fortunately for him, the commander had removed the power pack, which fits into the handle. And the power pack was just another one of those mysterious and innocuous looking items in the backpack that Shinak had no way to identify. After a close inspection of the commander's laser pistol, Shinak decided to carefully place it back into the preformed slot exactly as he found it. He then picked out a communicator, which was a solid, rectangular, black rubber-lined plastic device approximately twelve centimeters long. As he held it in his hand, he put pressure on the activating button, which produced a beep sound and a green LED light flash. He held the device closer for a better look when suddenly another beep sounded, and a red light flashed as the bright view screen popped on with Marie Chenault's face as her voice blurted out, "Come in, Commander."

This startled Shinak so much he dropped the communicator on the floor and backed away. As Marie's voice could be heard attempting to answer the call, Shinak stood gazing at the device on the floor. After three attempts to answer, Marie finally gave up, and the screen eventually went dark. The communicator once again rested silently. When Shinak felt safe enough to handle the device again, he bent down and gently picked it up, cradling it in both hands. He held it like a newly hatched baby bird, not applying any pressure. Just as he did with the laser pistol, he placed the communicator back into the backpack exactly as he found it. He then closed the commander's backpack, figuring out how the latches worked; he was meticulous in returning everything to its original state.

Shinak then walked through the opening into Gabriel's quarters. This time, he went directly to the wooden chest and removed Gabriel's backpack from it. He opened it quickly and noticed several objects that were similar to the commander's but a few which were different. Among those were the field glasses, which occupied about the same position in Gabriel's pack as the laser pistol did in the commander's pack. Shinak removed the instrument and stood up to examine it carefully. When he looked into the outer lenses, he could not see anything. Then he looked into the viewfinder. He was startled to see everything in the room that the glasses were pointed at enlarged twenty times. Shinak would lower the glasses and then raise them up again to his eyes several times until he realized that what he was seeing was the magnification of objects directly in front of him. He took them out onto the balcony to look at things and people in the palace garden and beyond. Then he pressed a soft switch on the top, which zoomed in the image to fifty times magnification, which again startled him, but he could not stop experimenting with the fascinating device.

As Shinak continued to look through the glasses, he was touching buttons that operated the recording and playback features. Suddenly, an image appeared in the viewfinder that was completely different from anything he was looking at. He was seeing the recorded images of the mesa battle that Gabriel recorded on the summit. Shinak was almost shaking as he watched his own soldiers being destroyed by the storm. When the recording ended, he was visibly shaken and disturbed by what he had seen. He composed himself enough to carefully return the field glasses to their place in Gabriel's pack and returned the pack to the chest exactly as he found it.

That night Shinak returned to the banquet hall but did not go inside himself. Instead, he found Tabar walking down a palace corridor and stopped him. Shinak asked Tabar to summon the king away from the banquet to give him some important information. Tabar agreed, so he walked in the back of the noisy banquet hall and approached the king. He moved very close to the king's head and crouched down to communicate in muted whispers. The king nodded, and then Tabar bowed and took his leave. About a minute later, the king rose from his seat, which prompted everyone else at the table to also rise. He graciously excused himself with a single short announcement.

"The duties of a king never cease."

King Malcor motioned to his chief advisor to come with him. They rose and walked out of the hall together.

It was a small and very private meeting held in an isolated and poorly lit antechamber. The small cadre consisted only of the king, Shinak, and the king's chief advisor. Shinak began his report as the king and his advisor stood captivated. When he described his experience with the field glasses, Shinak became very excited.

"They are miraculous. Distant objects appear closer. You can see people and things as if you were standing right in front of them but without being seen yourself."

The king nodded and commented, "A perfect tool for a spy."

Shinak agreed and then continued, "There is more, Your Majesty. Not only can these glasses see great distances but they can also see into the past and make it come alive again!"

"What do you mean?" the king inquired.

Shinak continued, "I looked into the glass again, and there I saw our soldiers and our Harite enemies in the desert on the mesa. I saw the storm come upon them. I watched everything happen right before my eyes as if I was there."

The chief advisor then spoke up. "This is sorcery and divination. We should have nothing to do with these things," he warned.

The king pondered for a moment and then asked who the glasses belonged to.

"I found it in the room of the dark-skinned one," Shinak answered.

The king nodded. "As I had suspected."

The chief advisor was puzzled. "Does Your Majesty believe him to be a spy?"

"I suspected it since I first saw him," the king answered.

Shinak's bearing then became stern and indignant.

"Your Majesty, give the order and I will have him arrested and executed."

The king began to pace back and forth. Then, speaking to them both, he answered, "No, they are foreign ambassadors, and we do not have enough proof. I believe the dark-skinned one gained the trust of the others to use their diplomatic mission as a cover so he could discover our weaknesses. Our enemies may be scoundrels, but they are clever."

Shinak then blurted out indignantly, "Then he must be arrested!"

But the king replied calmly, "He will be, but only when we find sufficient proof, then his companions will not be able to dispute his arrest. We cannot alienate these foreigners. They could be powerful allies."

Then the chief advisor came up with an idea.

"Your Majesty, what if we provide the proof for his companions to see?" he proposed.

The king listened intently.

"Continue," he said.

The king's advisor explained, "Last year we arrested a Harite spy in the city of Shekem. His accomplice managed to escape, but we found on him a map he was making of our cities, roads, military outposts, everything that could be of use to an enemy."

The king interrupted.

"Was he in league with any Amakite traitor?" he asked.

"He was tortured by fire, but we were not able to learn any more before he died," the advisor answered.

"So what is your plan?" the king asked.

The chief advisor continued, "We remain in possession of this map, and the descriptions upon it are written in the Harite language. Suppose this map were found in the possession of the dark-skinned foreigner. Could he then not rightfully be arrested as a spy?"

The king pondered for a moment, and then looking them both squarely in the eye, he ordered them to execute the plan.

It was about an hour after dawn the next morning. Clarendon and Gabriel were both still asleep in their own quarters. Five men were standing outside in the corridor; one was a palace butler who worked under Tabar and was responsible for cleaning the rooms and serving the needs of honored male guests and diplomats. With him were four palace guards each armed with a sword sheathed on a belt and holding a brass-tipped spear.

The butler moved quietly toward the door and opened it slowly. He saw Clarendon asleep on the bed and was turned toward the back wall. Then he crept through the opening into Gabriel's room. Gabriel was asleep almost facedown on the pillow. The butler moved to the foot of the bed while keeping his eye on Gabriel. The butler reached his hand under his cloak and pulled out the rolled up animal hide on which the Harite spy drew his map. He carefully laid it on the floor at the foot of Gabriel's bed. Then, as quietly and carefully as he entered, the butler made his way out undetected and closed the door gently behind him.

Outside the door, the butler stepped back as the four guards moved up to the door standing two by two. They stood silently for about one minute. Then suddenly, one guard banged on the door and then thrust it open. The two front guards rushed directly into Gabriel's room.

The other two positioned themselves with spears pointed at Clarendon, who rose up in his bed startled and confused. One of the guards shouted something at Gabriel, which woke him up only to find two spears pointed in his direction also.

After a few seconds, the butler, in a carefully planned performance, pointed down at the map on the floor by Gabriel's bed. A guard reached down to pick it up and unrolled it. He looked at it for a couple of seconds and then shouted an indignant question to Gabriel as he held it out for him to see. Gabriel did not understand all of the words, but he could see what was happening and chose to remain silent. Then the guard walked into Clarendon's room and held the map up for him to see, again saying something in an angry tone, but it was indiscernible to Clarendon. Clarendon pointed to the Universal Translator, which was left by itself on top of the wooden chest. But the guards positioned themselves so that neither one could get close to any of their equipment. The guards allowed Evans and Clarendon to finish dressing and put on their boots. Then they motioned with their spears for the men to walk out into the corridor in front of them.

Both men were under arrest for espionage and were being marched to the palace court for an impromptu hearing before the king.

Malcor was seated on his throne as the earthmen were brought before him. Commander Clarendon bowed deeply, but Gabriel nodded his head to the king while maintaining eye contact. It was a skeleton court, consisting only of the king, his chief advisor, Shinak, the butler as state's witness, and six more palace guards. The king began to speak to the earthmen in a low, calm voice. Gabriel understood some words, but missing some of the key words, he was not able to fully understand the question. Clarendon asked the king in English for his silver medallion, the Universal Translator, as he used hand motions around his chest where the device hung around his neck. The king understood and ordered one of the guards to bring it back quickly.

While waiting for the guard to return, the king conferred with Shinak in soft, muddled tones. Shinak then pointed to the guard who was in possession of the map. The king motioned for the guard to come forward. He did so, relinquishing the map to the king. They had a few brief words; after which the guard pointed directly at Gabriel. The king acknowledged and then ordered the guard to step back. Clarendon and Evans just looked at each other while the tension in the air grew thicker.

The few minutes it took for the guard to return with the Universal Translator seemed like an eternity, but finally he arrived with the shiny silver disc in his hand. He approached the king, who told him to hand it to Clarendon. The commander switched it on and put it around his neck. He then looked directly at the king and spoke.

"Thank you, Your Majesty," the commander said sincerely.

The king nodded and then started speaking. He addressed most of his remarks to Clarendon with an occasional glance toward Gabriel. He began his inquisition.

As the king explained the map to Clarendon, he was also allowing the commander a way to avoid being labeled an accomplice by suggesting that Gabriel deceived him as well. He proposed that Gabriel was at least partially Harite and that he won the confidence of the commander and his country to bring him with them on their mission. Clarendon told the king that he did not know of even the existence of such a map and that he knew Gabriel was not a spy. The difficulty for the commander was that he had completely fabricated a history and backgrounds for himself and his fellow explorers. Any alibi he could give had to be couched in that false reality. When this was considered, the king's ministers did have a case that could not be absolutely disproved.

King Malcor seemed determined to pass sentence on Gabriel, and Gabriel stood silently in a state of both shock and anger, saying nothing in his own defense. As the tension grew, the king sat back in his throne and spoke to Clarendon.

"To spy on a country to gain military advantage carries the penalty of death. This is true throughout the known world. However, since you have come to us as ambassadors of a distant country, I will be generous," the king said, revealing almost no emotion.

The commander was somewhat relieved, but anxiously awaited the king's next words. Malcor continued.

"He will be banned from our country forever. Since it is a three-day march to the sea where your ship is anchored, he will be given three days of food and water for the journey. He will not be permitted to take anything else with him. No Amakite will give him aid or comfort or even speak to him. If he is found again in our country after three days, he will die by fire at the feet of our god Balaak."

After passing sentence on Gabriel, King Malcor stood up as four guards encircled Gabriel. The court was officially concluded. Malcor walked toward Shinak to speak to him out of the hearing of the others. The king spoke softly.

"Have him followed from a distance. Let me know which way he goes," the king privately instructed Shinak.

Then as the guards were beginning to march Gabriel away, he turned to Clarendon for a last word as he was being escorted off.

"I'll say hello to *Archimedes* for you."

Gabriel was signaling to the commander that he intended to return to the shuttle. Clarendon felt that he had to play the part of a patsy who was taken in by Gabriel. The commander remained silent as the guards took Gabriel away. He could not argue with the king, and he certainly could not tell him the truth.

Early the next morning, four soldiers brought Gabriel outside the walls of the city. They slaughtered an animal related to the swine species and smeared a swath of blood across the back and chest of Gabriel's jumpsuit. This was to indicate to all Amakites that nobody was to help him, speak to him, or even get near him under penalty of death. The soldiers gave him two full skins of water and a pouch of food; all of which were attached by leather carrying straps. Gabriel slung the rations over his shoulders and looked back at the guards. One of the guards then shouted an angry word and pointed his finger southward toward the river. Without a word, Gabriel turned and walked away.

Gabriel followed the river in a generally southward direction, at least for as long as he was being observed, but he knew that soon he would have to turn east over the steep hills and into the canyon where the shuttle rested.

On the *Odyssey*, Marie Chenault had decided to take matters into her own hands. She would recall the shuttle by remote control. Since she had not heard from any of the landing party in more than forty-eight hours, her decision was to go down to the surface herself, taking Lea Moreno and Dr. Dunn with her.

Gabriel was not aware that he was being followed from a distance by the soldiers. At midmorning, Gabriel looked all around and saw nobody, so he turned eastward and started his climb up the steep, rocky slopes. When the soldiers saw Gabriel change course and head east, they reasoned to themselves that the accusations must have been true.

It was about midday when Gabriel reached the summit. The Tau Ceti sun was very warm and unfiltered by any clouds. Gabriel had already consumed half a skin of water on the climb. As he stood on the summit, looking out over the canyon, to his horror he saw the shuttle rising in the distance and then quickly disappearing into the sky. After some anxious thought, he reasoned that his short-term options were gone. He had to hope to find hospitable people in an inhospitable land. Gabriel began his reluctant journey into the vast eastern desert.

CHAPTER 10

THE SEARCH

By late afternoon, Gabriel was descending the eastern slopes of the range of rocky hills that separated the fertile valley from the barren desert. At that point, his one skin of water was only about one quarter full, and he had one other full skin left.

The desert floor was mostly flat, but strange rock formations, hills, and mesas filled the landscape as far as the eye could see. Gabriel decided to walk on flat, open ground to make the greatest distance with the least amount of water usage. He knew that somewhere in this region lived a nomadic people known as Harites. The limestone and sandstone formations created many natural caves both large and small. This desert could house a whole community of people almost without being detected unless one encountered them quite by accident. Obviously, the Harites had to manage to find enough food and water to survive.

Gabriel set as his goal to make contact with the Harites. His own survival depended on it. In spite of Malcor's description of them as primitive and warlike, Gabriel gambled that the laws of hospitality might be universal.

STAR TESTAMENT

The shuttle craft was securely docked onto the *Odyssey*. Marie Chenault, Dr. Dunn, and Lea Moreno were all preparing for departure. They wore their utility jumpsuits and rough-terrain boots. Each would take a communicator and a backpack loaded with provisions. This landing party was embarking on a search-and-rescue mission without any weapons or an electronic translator. However, Lea Moreno felt confident that she had learned enough of the Amakite language to get by, whereas Marie and the doctor only managed to learn a few key words.

More attempts were made to contact the commander, Sandra, and Gabriel but with no response. Marie's assumptions were correct regarding the first landing party's communicators and equipment: the Amakites had seized all of their equipment. Sandra and the commander were still being treated as honored guests in Malcor's palace, but they were also being carefully scrutinized until such time that the king felt confident that he could gain their allegiance.

Marie would not let her mind dwell on idle speculation regarding the fate of her companions; she was determined to find out. Her plan was to land the shuttle in the same canyon where it rested before. Dr. Dunn thought to bring a flare pistol with a good supply of phosphorus flares. It may be an impractical weapon, but it might at least frighten a primitive people. Marie commanded the expedition, but it was agreed that Lea would be the spokesperson due to her greater understanding of the Amakite language. After completing their thorough checklist, the shuttle departed for the planet's surface.

Commander Clarendon was summoned to a private meeting with the king. This informal gathering was to be set in the king's private residence within the palace. Shinak and two high-ranking military officers were with the king as well as several bodyguards and many servants in the background. Malcor could be forceful and ruthless when he felt it was necessary, and everybody knew that part of his nature could emerge at any time. But for the most part, Malcor was skilled in the use of charm and diplomacy in persuading people to see things his way. He spoke well and employed a direct but simple logic to his arguments. On this occasion, Malcor was attempting to persuade Clarendon to join him in his fight against his enemies.

The king offered Clarendon a home in Amakine or in any of the other cities of the kingdom. Furthermore, he was offered the rank of captain in the king's army and would be allowed to take possession of all his equipment again as long as it would be used in the king's service. Apart from the immediate wisdom of not refusing Malcor's offer, Clarendon was wanting for himself to play a more important role in the development of this world.

He was a naval commander, but the military back on Earth had evolved into something different than it had been historically. The military forces of the Earth were more of a worldwide police force under the control of a united world assembly, a world council, and a world court. The era of the sovereign nation state had melted away; therefore, wars between nations had become a thing of the past. But to guarantee this global stability, every activity of human beings was highly regulated and centralized. Religious freedom still existed, but only on a personal level and within licensed establishments of worship in which the government monitored and restricted any speech that was deemed political. So Commander Clarendon as well as the others on the expedition were all products of government conditioning.

Clarendon began to reason that Malcor's kingdom provided the best framework on this primitive planet to begin to establish a united and orderly world.

The commander took the evening to ponder over what the king had to say. As he walked outside the palace grounds, he noticed a large stone statue facing the avenue on the west side of the palace. It was the image of some Amakite military leader in full armor with sword and shield. The image stood about four meters high and was quite impressive. The commander found himself staring at it for several minutes as did some of the common natives as they walked along the avenue. Although he could not read the inscription under it, he was told by a helpful passerby that it was a statue of the Amakite warrior king who defeated the Harites and consolidated the Amakite Empire over a hundred years ago. King Malcor was said to be a direct descendent.

Clarendon stood in the street, spellbound by the heroic-looking image. As he contemplated his life and his purpose, he remembered a plaque with an anonymous inscription posted on his dormitory wall back at the academy. He recited it aloud to himself as he gazed at the statue.

"Few men have a chance for greatness. But great deeds are remembered. And being remembered makes us immortal."

The commander received a private audience with King Malcor that night. The forceful nature of Malcor's personality solidified with Clarendon's personal ambition to cause him to accept the king's offer. This time, it was not merely an act of expediency or deception. The commander did fully pledge himself to this cause with all his mind and heart.

The shuttle craft set down on the canyon floor just after dark. Marie planned to take the landing party over the summit at first light. Lea was in excellent physical condition, and she made the climb up to the summit like a professional. Marie was the oldest, but with her smaller frame and her many hiking and skiing trips throughout the European Federation, she also made the climb with very little difficulty. Dr. Dunn was several meters behind the women, moving slower and breathing heavier than he thought he should. Although healthy and physically strong, he did not have the cardiovascular stamina that the women had.

After about two hours, all three stood on the summit. They could see almost the entire valley, the river, and all five walled cities. Amakine was the largest and the closest. It was also the last known position of the other crew members. Amakine was their first destination; although none of the three could anticipate what kind of reception they would get from the inhabitants.

Gabriel reasoned that he had to make as many kilometers of progress on flat ground as he could before his water ran out. He marched solidly in the early morning and late afternoon into evening.

Fortunately, the desert had an abundance of caves and strange rock formations that could provide shelter from the midday sun. But after venturing about twenty kilometers into it, he found no water, no food, and no people. At that point he was reduced to only a half skin of water. Gabriel began to ponder the possibility of heading back to the river. While resting in a cave, he began to apply logic to his dilemma.

Half a skin of water was probably not enough, even with strict conservation, to march back twenty kilometers and make the long, hard climb over the hills and down to the river. Of course, even if he were to make it to the river, there was the risk of being captured and burned alive.

Gabriel knew that he could not remain anywhere in Malcor's kingdom. On the other hand, he asked himself why they recalled the shuttle. Could they be searching for him? But unless he stayed on open ground and they flew low enough, they would never see him. Still, the possibility remained, so Gabriel would look up to the skies many times a day. Logic dictated to proceed on his course to find the Harites.

The rescue party came upon the old stone bridge that spanned the eastern fork of the river. It was about two kilometers upstream from where the two forks converged and about one kilometer from the south gate of Amakine. The bridge was as old as the city walls and constructed of the same dense grey granite used in the walls. Its piers went down to bedrock, and it was wide enough to accommodate horse-drawn wagons as well as foot traffic. It was also high enough in the center to allow sailing vessels to pass under it. This was the bridge that the first landing party crossed to approach the city, finding it only after contemplating various other ways to cross the river. But Marie knew to head directly for it.

The fields surrounding the city seemed sparse with only a few Amakites visible in the distance. As they crossed over the bridge, they could see that the gates were wide open as they normally were during daylight hours. Marie led her party resolutely toward the city gates. As they approached the gates, two watchmen up on the wall saw them approach and were scrutinizing them with great interest. After observing the three strangers enter the city gates, one of the watchmen ran off to inform his superiors.

The strangely dressed visitors from Earth walked through the streets of Amakine. This landing party received a different reaction from the populous than did the first landing party. A friendly reception, rather than suspicion, greeted them mainly due to the fact that similar looking strangers that came before were the king's honored guests. Another factor was that none of these three had the darker skin color that Gabriel had, which caused most Amakites to be suspicious, although most did not know what happened to him.

Eventually, a small group of smiling, chatting Amakites started to follow the three around. This gave Lea the opportunity to try several Amakite greetings and phrases, which made the crowd even more excited. Some in the crowd were offering gifts such as elaborate beadwork or freshly cooked meat, which was a rare treat for the average Amakite. All three expressed great appreciation, but whereas Marie and Dr. Dunn mostly smiled and graciously received the gifts, Lea was speaking more and more fluently with the Amakites to the point where they actually started queuing up to speak with her for a minute or two.

After almost an hour of this excited attention, the crowd became very large with most of their interest centered on Lea. But suddenly, they became quiet and still as shouts could be heard from behind the assembly. The crowd began to separate in the middle and spread apart. A company of soldiers armed with shields and spears marched forward through the breech directly toward the landing party.

The soldiers stopped about three meters in front of them and spread out to surround them as the Amakite civilians moved back even farther. Lea attempted to speak to the soldiers, but not one of them answered her. Dr. Dunn started to remove his backpack to get his flare gun, but Marie told him to stop and just stand still. Then a voice could be heard approaching and issuing orders in Amakite; although it sounded electronically enhanced. The soldiers opened rank, and there stood Commander Clarendon in an opulent Amakite tunic, armor, sword of rank, and wearing the Universal Translator. His laser sidearm was in a holster hung on his waist on the opposite side from his sword. He wore a decorative breastplate made of polished silver and bearing the insignia of the king.

Gabriel was on his third day in his trek through the desert. His water was almost gone, and although he needed energy, he did not want to eat the remaining pieces of salt-dried meat and nuts that were in his pouch with so little water left. It was anxiety at that point, more than thirst or exhaustion, that plagued him. Questions began racing through his mind. How could a whole civilization be hidden? What if they did not live in the desert and just moved through it? Was this how it would all end for him? But then Gabriel composed himself long enough to think logically.

Up to that time, he had been walking predominantly eastward. But he remembered that a long range of high mountains lay far to the north. They were the probable source of the river. Of course, these mountains were several days away, but rivers and streams of water often flow for many kilometers from such a source. Perhaps the Harites lived closer to a water source originating from those distant mountains. Gabriel decided to turn and proceed due north.

He was hopeful but not optimistic that this course change would produce better results. It was a high probability that the river or any of its tributaries would swing eastward through the lower-elevation desert as it was followed to its source. Eventually, the Harites or some other group of people would settle around that important source of fresh water. But Gabriel was counting more on luck than the eventuality of finding water in several days. The reality was that he had about one more day of water left with strict rationing, one more day of limited travel after that without water, and then just one more day after that to live if he did not find water.

Gabriel pondered the beauty and mystery of the barren wilderness as the third day passed into night. He remembered the sudden windstorm that saved the Harites on the mesa.

Perhaps another sudden weather anomaly such as a rainstorm or flash flood might come to save him. Sometime during the night, Gabriel drank down his last swallow of water. He lay down under the clear open sky and went to sleep.

That night and the early morning were cooler than recent days. At first light, Gabriel got up and continued his search. The insulated jumpsuit that he wore, although heavily soiled and torn in spots, did protect him from extremes of heat and cold. It was also equipped with a chemical cooling system, which still worked reasonably well. That suit made it possible to get as far as he did in the desert, and he knew that without it, he would have succumbed to heat stroke or dehydration much earlier.

Gabriel marched on at a slow but steady pace. He kept his mouth closed and breathed through his nose so his mouth and throat would not dry out. As the day went on and grew warmer, he rested in the shade of the many large rocks that were scattered throughout this region. As the late afternoon approached, the Tau Ceti sun mercifully declined in the sky, leaving the desert bathed in a yellow-orange light. Gabriel felt his mouth and throat were becoming as dry as the sand and dusty dirt that he walked on.

Gabriel could only think of water. All other thoughts or philosophical musings vanished from his mind. It was pure instinctive focus on the immediate need for survival. As the sun declined still further, he felt as if his legs might collapse under him at any moment. But he continued to walk, for he knew that if he did stop, he might never get up again.

It was late afternoon, and the shadows were growing longer. Gabriel noticed a section of darker ground in a depression up ahead. He rubbed his eyes. Was it just a shadow or could it be moist ground? He moved closer and noticed that the soil was darker, and the dark soil seemed to form a broad line in the middle of a dry wash. When he reached it, he knelt down and grabbed a handful of the dirt. It was damp! With renewed strength, he followed the wet soil up the wash as it was getting deeper and wider. Eventually, he could see small puddles of water and then larger ones. He was tempted to drink from them right there, but if he could find moving water nearby, there would be less chance of contamination. And then he heard the faint sound of flowing water. It was about one hundred meters ahead, water flowing over rocks coming down from a flat rise.

With the last light fading, Gabriel made his way to the stream, put his head in the flowing water, and drank. Immediately the pain of his dry throat was gone. The water was cool, sweet, and life-giving. Gabriel drank all he could then began to fill his waterskins. He was standing in front of a rocky slope about five meters high. On top of the rise was a flat clearing, but he could not see into it very far. After a few more minutes of rest, he decided to attack the slope, which would have been a relatively easy task for anyone who was not so exhausted. As he crawled to the top he saw clearly. in the last bit of twilight, a tent.

It was a tent big enough to house about four people and was made of a tightly woven, coarse fabric. This tent was only about fifty meters away, but there were what seemed to be hundreds of other tents, along with several campfires, covering the desert floor. Gabriel could see some domestic animals, but no people close-by. He knew that he had finally found the Harite camp.

The stream meandered through the camp, and there were even patches of grass growing in several places. Gabriel was content with his situation for the time being. He resigned to place himself at the mercy of these people. But he was exhausted, and darkness was obscuring everything. Gabriel decided not to make his presence known until morning. So he found a small patch of tall grass nearby; he lay down on the grass and almost instantly fell asleep.

CHAPTER 11
THE HARITES

The bright dawn was not enough to awaken Gabriel from his deep and much needed sleep. Instead, it was the voice of a child, a young boy about the equivalent of eight Earth years old, that caught his attention. Gabriel opened his eyes and sat up. They momentarily startled each other as they made eye contact. The boy had a dark brown, almost copper skin tone, golden blond hair, and striking blue eyes.

After staring at Gabriel for a few seconds, the boy turned and ran back toward the tent shouting something indiscernible. Gabriel held his head as if in pain. He felt a moderate headache, which reached from his eyes to the back of his neck. So while the shadows were still long and the morning was still cool, he decided to lie back down and get a little more rest. But not long afterward, he became aware of another figure standing near him. Gabriel sat up. This time, it was a woman, and she held a sword down by her side.

She was an attractive woman who looked to be in her thirties. Her skin was also dark, her hair was a light brown, and she had gentle blue-green eyes. She wore a loose tunic of plain cloth with a colorful sash around her middle. The woman stood silently and watched Gabriel's every move. The boy stood just behind her, and he was also watching

Gabriel intently. She held the handle of the sword tightly but did not raise it up or threaten in any way.

Gabriel held up his hands open and clearly visible to the woman and boy to indicate that he was no threat. He began to use the Amakite word for *friend*, but quickly stopped himself. He decided not to speak any Amakite word, for he could not take a chance of alienating himself with these people. So Gabriel resolved to be himself and speak English. He knew that he would not be understood at first, but at least the unknown language of a strange foreigner might be received with less hostility than the language of a known enemy.

"Friend," he said in English with a sincere tone. The woman returned a puzzled glance, not quite knowing what to make of him. "Friend," Gabriel repeated, this time pulling his hands back in toward him. The woman then began to speak words that Gabriel could not understand. It sounded as though she was questioning him, which would be completely understandable given the circumstances. A few of the words she spoke sounded similar to some common Amakite words much the same way that some European languages of Latin origin share several similar-sounding words.

Gabriel rose to his feet. When he did, the woman took a step back and raised her sword in a ready position.

"No, no, it's all right!" Gabriel said with his hands open. "I mean you no harm."

Gabriel tried to communicate more with tone of voice, facial expressions, and body language than with words. The woman slowly lowered her sword again back down to her side. He pointed southward out toward the desert, and with hand motions and some theatrics, he tried to describe his journey through the desert, his search for water, and the Harite camp. He handed her his food pouch. When she looked inside and saw only a couple of pieces of dried meat and a few nuts left, her demeanor became more of compassion and trust for him.

She motioned for him to follow her as they walked toward her tent. The woman and the boy walked into the tent, but Gabriel hesitated until she turned back and said something to him with a hand motion inviting him inside. Gabriel noticed a stone fire pit outside with a bronze frame over it that supported a large copper cooking pot. He noticed similar fire pits outside most of the tents haphazardly scattered throughout the desert floor.

Gabriel walked inside the tent half-expecting to see her husband or other family members. But the tent had no other people in it. The tent was large enough to house four or five people. It was simple but clean, having a canvas floor with colorful wool rugs spread about to sit or lie on.

The woman asked Gabriel to sit down while she went over to a wooden box at one corner of the tent. She set down the sword and opened the lid on the box, pulling out a large, round loaf of dark whole-grain bread. She pulled apart a piece of bread that more than filled her hand. Almost instantly Gabriel smelled the mouthwatering aroma of the fresh bread. She handed the piece to Gabriel for which he sincerely thanked her with words and a slight bow of the head. Then she broke off another slightly smaller piece for the boy and a smaller piece for herself. All three were sitting on the floor facing one another. When Gabriel bit into the bread, he was amazed first by how delicious it was but then by how remarkably filling it was. He was very hungry, but that one piece of bread was as satisfying to him as a banquet.

Gabriel took the opportunity to learn more about the Harites. He held up his remaining piece of bread and pointed to it. "Bread," he said in English. The woman stared at him a moment, and then she said, "Lekem." Gabriel repeated it, and the woman nodded in the affirmative. Gabriel was pleased that the woman was willing to teach him some Harite words. He was also happy that the Harite and Amakite languages were similar in many ways, for the Amakite word for bread was *lekeem*.

Then the boy walked over to Gabriel, hoping to get a closer look at his jumpsuit. The boy rubbed his hand on the silky, padded material of the arm and shoulder while holding his unfinished bread in the other hand. Gabriel was getting a bit self-conscious because his suit was dirty, heavily worn, had dried bloodstains on it, and probably smelled.

"Yakob!" the woman shouted, which made the boy stop and draw back.

"Yakob?" Gabriel asked, pointing to the boy.

The boy nodded in the affirmative and then sat back down. Gabriel then pointed to his own chest and said, "Gabriel." The woman and the boy looked at him but said nothing. Then Gabriel repeated the action. Finally, the woman spoke Gabriel's name back to him with a hint of a smile. Gabriel pointed at the woman. At first she did not respond but shortly realized that he wanted her name. She placed her hand to her upper chest and said softly, "Miram."

Commander Clarendon brought Marie, Lea, and Dr. Dunn into the palace, and before long they were given an audience with the king. Malcor was particularly taken by Lea. Not only was she attractive and shapely, but she spoke enough Amakite to make her very popular with the court. The doctor and Marie spoke very little for themselves; most of their answers came from the commander, who was increasingly gaining the trust of the king.

Their appearance before the king had been more of a diplomatic welcoming than an inquisition. But following that, after learning about Gabriel's fate, Marie pressed the commander to launch a search. The commander told Marie and Dr. Dunn that Gabriel was last seen heading east into the desert and that he did not have his communicator or any of his equipment with him. Clarendon authorized Chenault and Dunn to take the shuttle and conduct a search. If they found Gabriel alive, they were to return to the ship with him and stay there until further notice. He also added that they should not interact with any of the desert people.

Dr. Dunn questioned Clarendon on this last order but received a terse response. The commander cited the fact that they did not speak the language but, more importantly, that he believed the desert dwellers to be violent and warlike and that the two of them were unarmed. Concerning the third point, Dunn proposed that Clarendon allow them to borrow the laser sidearm. But the commander emphatically refused, stating that he was a captain in the king's army. With that, Dunn simply said, "I see," then he and Marie turned and walked down the main corridor. As they neared the outer doors of the palace, Dunn could not help commenting to Marie, "The man is bloody delusional."

Marie made no comment. At the king's request, Lea was to remain in the palace, a decision that was entirely acceptable to her.

The hours of the day seemed to fly by quickly for Gabriel. Not only was he enjoying the hospitality of Miram and her son, Yakob, but he was learning much about the Harite language, their culture, and even some of the personal history of his host. Miram had a husband, Yakob's father, who was a soldier, as most Harite men were called on to be as the need arose. He was killed in a skirmish about two years prior. They allowed the widow to keep his sword.

According to Harite law, every able-bodied male between about twenty and forty years old had to train as a soldier. They could live at home and engage in their own profession. But they had to be ready on short notice to join their unit and fight any enemy that the elders and judges directed them to.

The Harites had no king. They were governed by a council of elders, who were actually elected by the men in each district to serve a term of one year. The major laws and instructions for the people were given to the council by the priests who claimed to receive them directly from their god. The council, in turn, appointed judges to settle disputes and enforce the laws throughout the districts. A supreme military commander was named by the priests upon direct instructions from their god.

The Harites were a clannish people to whom family and the perpetuation of family were very important. A young man who was newly married would be excused from participating in battle for one year so that he may have the opportunity to sire offspring. If a man died and his wife had not borne any children, the law required the man's brother or closest male relative to take the woman into his house and make her his wife to bear children and continue the bloodline. If the woman had at least one child when her husband died, then the brother's obligations went from mandatory to voluntary. In Miram's case, her brother-in-law had a younger and much more possessive wife, so he just did not offer Miram and her son a place in his home.

As the day stretched on, Gabriel learned many Harite words from Miram, who seemed to take pleasure in teaching him her language. At some point, Yakob became bored and went outside to play. The Harites and Amakites did have several words that derived from common origins, but there were also many words that were completely different. Through words, sign language, and various means of visual description, Gabriel was able to ascertain a rough history of the Harites.

It seems that centuries earlier, their patriarch, Akran, lived with his family and clan in the mountains far to the north. In fact, the name Harite in their language means "mountain people," even though they have been forced to live in the desert for nearly one hundred years.

The story goes that one day their god spoke to Akran and told him to move with his entire clan southward to the river valley. On their way, Akran's people encamped on the shores of the Sea of Ofir, which is in reality a large lake created by the river's eastern tributary. This lake was bordered by hills on the east and west, desert on the north, and the fertile valley to the south. After a year, Akran's people began to prosper along the lake region. Grazing was good, so their animal herds grew. They traded with the local people and increased their wealth.

Then the king, who controlled three cities in the northern valley as well as all of the neighboring countryside, demanded tribute from the Harites. The king dispatched three thousand soldiers to collect the tribute, which was one-third of their livestock, crops, gold, and anything else of value they had. Akran only had about five hundred fighting men, so he inquired of his god whether he should pay the tribute or fight. Akran's god told him to attack the king's army in the dark of night.

When the king's envoy demanded an answer, Akran's reply was to delay.

"You will have my answer by morning," he said.

That night, while the women and children kept the fires lit in the Harite camp, the men crept up the hillside to the soldiers' camp. When they had surrounded the camp, they let out a loud yell and attacked the camp from all sides. Even though only about half of Akran's five hundred men had any type of real weapon, they fought ferociously. Some of the men had only crudely made clubs and axes; others used farming tools. But they took the king's soldiers by complete surprise. The confusion and the slaughter were complete. By dawn, the few soldiers of the king that remained alive were scattered to the winds. Not one of Akran's men lost his life in the attack.

Over the years, the Harites settled more of the valley as their numbers, strength, and wealth grew. From time to time the Harites would be attacked by indigenous warlords or by people of the west wanting to stake claims in the well-watered valley. But each time, the Harites, with the miraculous help of their god, not only defeated their enemies but became masters of all their territory. Eventually, the Harites took control of the whole valley, which ranged from the Sea of Ofir to the Great Sea and from deep into the western hill country to the eastern desert.

Akran is said to have followed his god all his life until he finally died an old man and was buried in secret. His sons and grandsons became judges over the people. Akran had destroyed the public idols, which the Amakites and other indigenous people had erected to their gods. He also began to build the great walls around the cities, a task that his sons had to complete.

For three hundred years the Harites governed their land justly, and all of the people prospered. But eventually, the people and their leaders forgot their god and his laws. Amakite idols were reappearing everywhere, and even many Harites were worshipping them with their Amakite neighbors.

A prophet named Shomash arose to proclaim his god's judgment upon the Harites. In a very short time, a nomadic people known as the Magar swept in from the west. They made a secret alliance with the Amakites and together attacked and defeated the Harites. Thousands were killed, and those that remained took refuge in the Great Desert.

After taking all the spoils they could carry, the Magar eventually left the valley in the firm control of the Amakites. Shomash proclaimed that God would preserve and test his people in the desert for a hundred years until even the memory of all those who had rebelled against him had been extinguished, or so the legend goes.

Gabriel wanted to go out among the Harites to study their culture firsthand. This was an anthropologist's dream, and he was living it. Miram had been enormously helpful in his understanding of the

Harites, but it was just a beginning. Gabriel found himself becoming very attracted to Miram in many different ways, and he felt comfortable in her presence. But he tried to suppress any outward demonstration of those feelings.

As the Cetian sun was setting and the western sky morphed to red, Gabriel looked out of the tent opening to find a nearby patch of grass where he would spend another night. As he gazed around outside, he thought he noticed a silvery glimmer speeding across the sky toward the south. Could it be the shuttle? Were they searching for him? he wondered. He knew that if they continued a low-altitude search that they might eventually see the Harite camp and land nearby. At that point Gabriel had mixed feelings about being rescued.

Gabriel arose with the sunrise from his grassy bed. Miram was up even earlier and came out to offer him more bread and goat's milk for breakfast. He let Miram know that he wanted to visit the Harite camp that day. Miram offered to accompany him, which Gabriel gratefully accepted. Yakob finally woke up and decided to tag along.

They followed the stream that meandered through the camp, passing hundreds of tents and a few crude dwellings of stone or sod. The tents were not spaced closely or uniformly such as would be expected in a military camp. Instead, they were haphazardly spaced with room enough for gardens and grazing areas for a small number of animals. The stream flowed with greater volume as they reached the center of the camp. Gabriel was curious to see the source of such abundant water in the middle of a vast desert.

It was clear that the Harites must have numbered in the tens of thousands just from what was visible from his vantage point. Walking past many Harites going about their daily work, Gabriel received a few curious stares from some, but most went about their business.

As the three of them continued to walk upstream, a noise of rushing waters could be heard in the distance. The camp was scattered in the flat ground and caves among the rocky hills of the desert. When the stream turned and they moved around an enormous granite boulder, Gabriel at last saw the source of the stream. It was a powerful flow of gushing water that poured out of the middle of one of the rocky hills.

Since these hills were not part of a high range of mountains, this amazing water source would have had to flow underground for more than a hundred kilometers. It could be the outlet of an underground river or perhaps an artesian well. But logically, the terrain did not seem to support either theory. Yet there it was, strange, out of place, but very welcome.

Another stream could be seen emanating from the same source, and this one seemed to run through the north end of the camp. The Harites had made several crossing points in each stream by placing large rocks in a line across the stream about one pace apart. The large clearing between the streams was used as a community meeting center and marketplace. A well-constructed stone bridge spanned each stream leading into the central marketplace. This focal point of the camp was bustling with activity as the people gathered to buy and sell, trade or just socialize.

Gabriel was making many mental notes as he walked down the long row of merchants selling their wares. Miram and Yakob followed close behind. Then a garment merchant who noticed Gabriel suddenly yelled out to him. Gabriel stopped. The man was pointing down at Gabriel's boots, which were insulated rugged-terrain boots made of synthetic materials. The merchant was very interested in the boots and pointed to some handmade leather sandals, a cotton tunic, and a dark red woolen robe, which he offered in trade. Gabriel understood the offer even though he did not understand every word the merchant said.

After thinking about it, he decided that blending in with a society would make his work and life a lot easier than standing out from it. He nodded yes. Just then, Miram spoke up. She was speaking to the merchant and pointing to another item, a crimson-colored sash that would go nicely with the robe. The merchant at first argued. But Miram proved to be a tough negotiator. He gave in and agreed to include the sash with the deal. As the merchant assembled the goods, Gabriel looked to Miram and whispered "Thank you" in the Harite language; to which Miram nodded and smiled.

So Gabriel removed his boots and demonstrated to the merchant how the pressure fasteners opened and closed. The merchant felt that he could get top price for this very strange but very practical footwear. Gabriel made it known that he wished to change into his new clothes, so the merchant allowed him to go behind his tent. Gabriel wanted to burn his jumpsuit, but it would not burn, so he stashed it under a rock then shortly emerged from behind the tent looking like a true Harite.

CHAPTER 12
TRANSFORMATION

King Malcor was quite experienced at rewarding those who pleased him and punishing those who did not. Robert Clarendon became a trusted officer in the king's service not only because of the miraculous technology that he had command of but more so because Clarendon began to link his own destiny to that of the king's. He saw the king not only as a benefactor but as a means to spread civilization and government to a primitive and anarchistic world.

Lea Moreno willingly became a favorite companion of the king. She was known to have spent the last several nights in the king's private chambers. In addition to her obvious physical attributes and her seductive power over men, she could also carry on intelligent discussions with Malcor in his own language, a quality that he found to be rare in the women of his own culture. Rumors were being whispered about the court that the king would soon take Lea as his wife, making her the new queen of the Amakites.

Sandra Hirata had, to some extent, aroused the desire of King Malcor before Lea arrived. But out of respect for a fictitious foreign king, Malcor made no overtures toward Sandra except to treat her as an honored royal guest. Recently, she visited the other cities of the valley, where she learned much of the Amakite language and culture. But without explanation, Clarendon never returned her personal communicator to her.

The governor of the city of Jeku was a young man who inherited his wealth and office from his father who had died about a year earlier. The young governor became very attracted to Sandra, and as the days passed, she became attracted to him. He had a handsome, boyish face, but he also quickly perceived Sandra's intellect and independent nature, which he found fascinating. Sandra would walk around the city streets with him and discuss urban planning and how they might install plumbing and sewage systems to improve sanitation. The governor was genuinely open to her ideas, but he was also careful to avoid any sexual advances or suggestions of marriage until he could be sure they would be welcome. Of course, Sandra also understood where all of this was leading. In this world, it was not acceptable for a young woman to remain unattached for a long time, no matter what her rank.

At last Marie Chenault and Dr. Dunn discovered the Harite camp. They landed the shuttle behind a small hill within a short walking distance from the outskirts of the camp. They reasoned that if Gabriel was still lost in the desert, he would most likely be dead by now, but he might still be alive if he found the Harite camp and they gave him sanctuary.

Dr. Dunn was becoming more bold and aggressive in his willingness to take risks. He started to regularly wear a holster that carried the flare pistol and six cartridges. Marie was softening towards him both emotionally and physically. These two members of the expedition had the least interaction so far with the inhabitants of this world. As a result, they came closer together in purpose as they perceived themselves more as the guardians of the original mission. But this was becoming increasingly difficult as authority and allegiances became more blurred. The doctor and Marie were both becoming more apprehensive with the commander's increasing alliance with Malcor. The doctor brought up the subject much more often than Marie did; although it could be inferred that she was thinking along the same lines.

Most of the natives of Ceti 2 made their living through subsistence farming and or by raising livestock. However, a minority became skilled tradesmen in a variety of needed professions. As the days passed, Gabriel looked for an honorable way to support himself among the Harites. He felt that he could no longer impose on Miram's kind nature, nor could he just move in with her, for such a thing was considered unseemly to these people. But Miram had a younger brother named Lemek, who was a metal worker. He had three children, but none were old enough to help him at the forge. So Miram made the introduction, and Gabriel agreed to work for food, a place to stay, and a few pieces of silver whenever the items they made would sell at market. The arrangement worked out well for all concerned.

Metallurgy for the people of this region primarily utilized copper, brass, or bronze. The smelting of iron or steel was not known at that time. Gabriel had to pump the primitive bellows made from animal hide to heat the fire in the stone forge hot enough to shape a piece of metal into any useful item, from a sword to an oil lamp. It was cutting-edge technology for this culture, and Gabriel was determined to learn it and then to advance it.

One day, while taking a break from work, Gabriel and Lemek were resting when Lemek's wife brought them some food and shared a little gossip. Rumors were spreading through the camp about two strangers, one man and one woman, who were walking around the camp. They had white skin and were strangely dressed. A judge tried to question them, but they could not speak or understand the words. When Gabriel heard this and registered the fact that these two strangers could well be his shipmates, he rose to his feet and asked the woman if she knew where they were last seen. The woman only knew that they were somewhere on the north end of the camp, which was a walk of several kilometers. Gabriel told the metalsmith and his wife that he might know these strangers and asked to be excused to try and find them. Lemek reluctantly agreed. So Gabriel marched north at a rapid pace to make it before sundown.

Dr. Dunn and Marie were being carefully watched not only by common Harites, but by tribal officials armed with swords and spears.

They were trying to maintain a harmless and friendly presence, but their clothing and equipment along with their ignorance of the Harite language were becoming real handicaps. As they tried to move away from the gathering crowds, many Harites would follow them with even more onlookers joining in.

It reached the point where Dr. Dunn felt that he and Marie were being surrounded and threatened. He reached into his belt pouch for a flare cartridge and then quickly snapped it into the flare gun. Marie was whispering to him to stop. But this time the doctor continued. He aimed the flare gun straight up toward the sky and fired. The flare shot up high and became a bright white glowing ball that hung in the air for several seconds.

The crowd instantly moved back. Many were afraid; some screamed. Gabriel saw the flare and ran toward it. He worked his way through the disorganized circle of Harites that surrounded Marie and the doctor. When Gabriel stood in front of them, they both had to take a moment to register in their minds that this was their former crew member. By this time, not only was Gabriel wearing Harite clothes but his hair was growing longer, and the whiskers on his face were growing out into a full beard.

His companions were genuinely happy to see him as they shook hands, and Gabriel gave them a quick, condensed version of his experiences. Meanwhile, the crowd of Harites stood watching, more curious than ever. Then two armed officers approached Gabriel. When they ascertained that he could understand and speak their language reasonably well, they ordered all three to accompany them to the local judge. They were to be questioned again, but this time with Gabriel to serve as interpreter.

The Harite judge held court in a high but shallow sandstone cave. Spectators were not allowed to loiter around. Only persons who had disputes or who were accused of crimes could enter. The judge had one scribe to record his judgments and four armed guards to execute his judgments.

Gabriel was becoming nervous at the prospect of once again being interrogated by a high official who held the power of life or death over him. The judge was a middle-aged Harite man with a gentle but serious face. His bench was a large flat stone set near the back wall of the cave. When the judge took his seat, he looked at Gabriel and began his questioning.

"Tell us who you are and how you know these strangers."

By the tone and substance of the judge's question, Gabriel was convinced that he was truly being accepted as a Harite and a member of their community. His apprehension began to melt away.

Gabriel decided early on that deceit and fabricating stories might sometimes be of short-term benefit, but it could eventually lead to disaster if the lie is discovered. He believed that he was not as quick and clever as the commander was. Gabriel resolved to be as honest as he could within the limits of these people's understanding and acceptance.

He explained to the judge that he and his friends had journeyed from a far-off land in which people of different tribes and races all live and work together. The judge listened with interest. Gabriel went on to explain that he first came to the Amakite country, but the king thought that he might be a Harite, so Malcor exiled him. He fled into the desert. After four days of wandering and with his water gone, he found the Harite camp almost by accident. Gabriel pointed back to the doctor and Marie then explained to the judge that his two loyal friends went out to the desert to search for him, and now they are united again.

The judge seemed to be moved by Gabriel's story, and somehow he discerned the truth of it. He ruled that all three were released to go or stay and live among them, whichever they chose. Not only were Gabriel and his companions exonerated, but in the days to come they were introduced to many prominent Harites including a few of the ruling elders.

The doctor and Marie were treated with hospitality by most of the Harites, but they were slow to learn the language and to blend in with the Harite society. They continued to wear their survival jumpsuits and carry their equipment wherever they went. Marie would often pull out her multiscanner to test for different forms of energy. Occasionally, when she conducted her tests in view of some unsuspecting Harites and the display screen would show bright wave patterns, she would get many puzzled looks directed her way.

Gabriel was also engaged in learning more about the Harites, but from his perspective as more of an insider than an outsider. At that point, he had almost free rein in the camp. All three of the expedition members suspected that the Harites controlled or at least benefited from some technology or force that protected them, sustained them, and held them all together. None of the three had yet spoken to any of the priests, who might give them more insight. And of course, there was the reclusive, aging prophet Tumalek, who lived in a cave just outside of camp and would appear, the Harites said, only when he was to deliver a special word or instruction from God to the people.

Tumalek could well be the key to the secret of the Harites. Marie once speculated, only half-seriously, that Tumalek might be sitting in his cave at a control panel that operated powerful alien machinery that, in turn, controlled the natural forces of this planet. Gabriel took this theory much less seriously than Marie or the doctor. He had studied what his instructors called myths and legends of ancient civilizations on Earth. Historically, the strange natural events, if true, could not conclusively be traced to advanced technology. Still, as Gabriel's search for answers continued, his bonding with the Harite people grew stronger.

CHAPTER 13

THE GREAT CRUSADE

Amakine bristled with excitement and color as maidens threw flower petals out onto the streets by the basketful. Malcor decreed that Lea would become his wife and queen over his kingdom. Lea was an ambitious woman, and she believed that she had found her calling in life. The people openly showed great affection for her. It was hard to determine for sure how much of their enthusiasm for the future queen was genuine and how much was simply the desire to remain in favor with the king. Clarendon was privately apprehensive about the prospect. As his status as one of the king's high-ranking officers increased, his communication and control over the other members of the expedition decreased. Now, one of his crew members was soon to become his superior. Still, both Clarendon and Lea had resolved to make the most out of their lives in the world they found themselves in and to make their own indelible marks upon it.

    A royal procession was scheduled, which would start with a show of military might. War chariots would lead the way, carrying the king's top-ranking officers, including Robert Clarendon. Following that would be a cavalry unit in which the horses were covered in scale armor, and the riders wore polished brass helmets. About two thousand men marched behind. These represented the king's best troops, consisting of archers, lancers, and infantry.

Lea was the focal point of the parade. She rode in an open wagon pulled by two magnificent but slow moving white horses. Four young maidservants dressed in white linen were also in the wagon. They knelt down around Lea to attend to her every need. Twelve teenage girls, also dressed in white, were holding baskets of flower petals, which they threw into the air as they danced ahead of the wagon. The wagon itself was a flat custom-built platform with solid gold stanchions around the perimeter with eyeholes at the top. A solid gold chain was strung through the eyeholes to act as a barricade. The outside edges of the platform were covered with colorful flowers and green vines. There was no driver's seat; instead two handlers would walk the horses and guide the wagon.

Lea herself wore a low-cut white gown with a multijeweled gold necklace and gold bracelets. She wore a light wreath of flowers on her head. Lea waved and smiled as the crowds yelled, screamed, and cheered when she passed by. A contingent of the palace guard marched behind the wagon and, behind them, several priests dedicated to the god Molak who were chanting and burning incense. The sight of these priests was puzzling to some people. Of course, they expected to ask for the blessings of the gods upon this wedding and their new queen, but the strange thing about it was that Molak was the god of war.

The ceremony was held in the palace court. As usual, only nobles and high officials could be inside the palace. Sandra Hirata and the governor were among the invited guests. The great doors were left open as the common people filled the palace garden and overflowed around the outer gate. When the ceremony was complete, the priests removed the flower wreath from Lea's head and placed on it a crown of gold studded with red and white jewels. Malcor took Lea's hand and stood next to her facing his subjects. The whole city of Amakine then bowed to their new queen.

The wedding seemed to impart a sense of unity among the Amakites. Malcor wasted no time in exploiting these feelings by doubling the taxes on his people from one-tenth to one-fifth of all the increase of crops, livestock, and the trading in gold, silver, and precious gems. In addition, he decreed that all able-bodied young men report to their local military camp to be trained and enrolled as soldiers subject to active duty at any time.

The governor of Jeku was technically exempt because of the office he held, but he could serve in the military as a high-ranking officer with all the corresponding authority and privileges connected with it even though he had no military experience. The young governor was seriously contemplating this course of action in spite of Sandra's strong objections. He thought that this move would bring him more in favor with the king and with the people. But with his own wedding planned for the near future and Sandra's strong opposition, he finally relented. Sandra could sense what was coming, and she did not like it at all. King Malcor, no longer content with consolidating his power, sought to expand it.

Malcor convened his war council in secret. Shinak and a few other high-ranking officials and military officers were in attendance. Robert Clarendon was also there, about twelve men in all. Queen Lea was absent; in fact, she was not even aware of the meeting. The king's intentions were clear and not subject to discussion. He demanded the complete subjugation or destruction of the Harites. Shinak had convinced the king that the strange devices that Commander Clarendon had control of could give them a strategic advantage over their enemy and would overcome the power of their god.

Clarendon had possession of the communicators and all of the equipment that once belonged to Gabriel, Lea, and Sandra as well as his own. He also knew that the doctor, Marie, and Gabriel were among the Harites.

For the last few days, Marie had inadvertently given Clarendon valuable intelligence concerning the Harites. Although she could not say much about their military strength since most soldiers were civilians until they are called into service, Clarendon could get Marie's exact position from her transmissions that gave him the location of the Harite camp. Clarendon also extrapolated out of Marie's communications that the Harites had no walls, stockade, or fixed defenses around the camp. He was careful to extract as much information from Marie as he could without disclosing his intent. The last communication the commander had with Marie was to order her to take the doctor and Gabriel back to the *Odyssey* and await further instructions. Marie acknowledged the order but privately decided that she would get around to it in her own time.

The king and Shinak placed high expectations on Clarendon to be able to give the Amakite army advantages that could not be overcome by any natural or supernatural forces; of the latter the commander never believed in. Clarendon was named supreme commander of the expedition, and he took it to heart.

The king had decided that the Great Crusade, as he called it, would begin in seven days. Of course, only a few of his closest advisors realized that this was only the opening salvo in his scheme to build an empire. Lea knew that she had the admiration of the people and the ear of the king. She was as manipulative and ambitious as Malcor himself; although she was not aware of all the details of his plans. She saw herself as being well on the road to becoming the most powerful woman on the planet.

Clarendon spent two days training his best three scouts in the use of communicators, and one was given the field glasses to spot enemy troop movements. When the soldiers finally quelled their fascination over these devices, they simply followed instructions on how to operate them and became very competent. The scouts were sent out three days in advance of the army and were ordered to take positions on hilltops approximately midway between the Sea of Ofir and the Harite camp.

The day before the troops would move out was a day of high celebration in each of the five major cities of the valley. Each city had its own statue of Molak in or near the central square. Lea was now fully aware of the upcoming military expedition, as were most of the Amakites. She volunteered to take center stage at the festivities around the statue of Molak. The people gathered in the streets in a display of heady nationalism. Lea, of course, downplayed the graphic calls for Harite blood and ignored the Amakite tradition of setting aside several surviving enemy captives to be bound and thrown alive into a fire pit before Molak.

Clarendon did not participate in these activities. Instead, he spent the day preparing himself and his troops for their march through the streets of Amakine on their way into the eastern desert. The commander was personally repulsed by many aspects of pagan barbarism, but he said or did nothing against it, reasoning that it would just be a temporary phase on the way to planetary unity.

The Amakites had a small navy consisting of twenty-four ships that Malcor and his predecessors purchased over the years from a seafaring people known as the Selecians. These ships were similar in design and construction to the ancient Greek triremes. Each ship was of wood construction, about thirty-five meters in length. They had one mast with one square sail placed in the forward third of the ship. The main purpose of these ships was to carry the king's troops up and down the river system and to patrol the kingdom from the lake known as the Sea of Ofir all the way down to the river delta where it merges with the Great Sea. Each vessel could transport about two hundred soldiers, who would also serve as oarsmen. Three tiers of oars extended from each side of the hull to power the ship when the wind was calm.

All twenty-four ships were to be used to transport the troops, which were based in the cities and villages near the southern and western shores of the lake, to the rocky and barren eastern shore. The larger force would march northeast into the desert and rendezvous with the troops from the ships in a flat, desolate area known as the Plain of Zofar.

Dr. Dunn and Marie did not find it necessary to return to the shuttle craft for provisions over the last several days. They would always find Harites willing to share food with them and give them a place to sleep. The doctor had on several occasions treated injuries and illness among the people in the camp. Even with the limited medical supplies and drugs in his field kit, he was far more effective in healing and relieving suffering than were the Harite home remedies. As a result, the doctor and Marie were welcomed throughout the camp, even though they still struggled with the language.

By this time, Gabriel was fluent in the Harite language; although most of the Harites that knew him realized that he was a foreigner.

Gabriel returned to Lemek, the blacksmith, and resumed his work. He talked Lemek into allowing him to work on a project that would greatly improve the efficiency of the forge.

The idea was to use some of the scrap bronze and brass to construct a foot-operated fan blower for the forge. The blower would be installed in the side stone wall of the forge near the top and would replace the cumbersome and less effective bellows above. To Gabriel, it was a matter of simple mechanics, but to Lemek, it was an odd puzzle that Gabriel was piecing together. Certainly, it was not like anything this culture had ever seen. Still, Lemek was fond of Gabriel and allowed him to work on the project after their daily work was finished.

An unexpected distraction began to come about for Gabriel. Teenage girls would go out of their way to stroll past Lemek's place and the forge where Gabriel worked. Most of them were at or approaching sexual maturity for that culture, and they knew that Gabriel was not married, so an intelligent and handsome stranger was attractive to them. Some of the girls would cinch in their tunics at strategic points to reveal their shape. Lemek and his wife both knew well what was happening, and Gabriel soon learned for himself. These girls were looking for a husband.

In the Harite culture, marriage and a lifetime commitment were a prerequisite to sex and the starting of a family. It was expected that the girl could make herself noticed by the man she was interested in. But it was the man who could choose the girl and then make arrangements with her family for the marriage. Since Gabriel was neither ready to make such a commitment nor willing to become outcast by the people who had taken him in, he would smile at the girls as they walked by then turn his face back to his work.

It was just after dawn when the trumpets sounded throughout the camp. They began in the distant northern end of the camp then were picked up and relayed by various trumpeters to be sure that the entire camp was alerted. The purpose could be a warning of some kind, a call to war, or a call to an assembly. All able-bodied Harite men were required to answer the call. Strangers and foreigners were not required to go unless they married into the Harite tribe. Gabriel asked Lemek if he could go with him. Lemek agreed, so the two packed some bread and carried waterskins for their long walk to the far end of the camp.

As they neared the north end of the camp, the crowd of people became denser. About that time, Gabriel looked up and noticed yet another strange weather anomaly. A single dark cloud hung low in the sky over a particular spot. And even though it billowed and swirled, it did not move with the wind. This was the only cloud visible in the sky at that time. Under the cloud, a man could be seen in the distance, standing on a large rock part of the way up the slope of a hillside.

Gabriel could not identify the man on the rock, but he was told that it was Tumalek, the prophet. He had already begun to speak, and the crowd was quieting down to the point that not even a whisper could be heard among them. There was naturally good acoustic amplification from the hill on which he stood. But for those not close enough to hear, there were trusted district leaders who would restate the entire message afterward. The summation of the message delivered by Tumalek to the people could be translated as follows:

"Listen carefully to all of the words of your god. The Amakites have again risen up against you. Have no fear. You will again go out against them and drive them back. I will go before you and give you the victory. Send only one thousand of your best warriors to meet them at the Plain of Zofar, and there you will see that it is the power of your god, and not numbers, that will save you. The time approaches for you to return to the land that I have given you. Soon the stream of waters that I have provided will stop flowing. That will be the sign for you to fold up your tents and gather your possessions to leave your homes here in the desert and march toward the river valley. When your warriors reach the summit of the hills overlooking the valley, I will send fire from the sky to destroy the city of Amakine. When the inhabitants of the valley see this, they will tremble with fear. They will surrender to you and be placed under your rule."

When the aging prophet concluded his address, some of the elders went up to help him down the hill and escort him back to his home. The mysterious cloud then moved over the center of the camp. A tumult of noise and excitement soon overtook the people.

Lemek knew that he was not among the tribe's best warriors, so he was to go home, make weapons, and stand by with his local unit to defend the camp if necessary. Gabriel was much more anxious. He did not have the faith that most of the Harites had. He looked up at the cloud and remembered that these people had some fantastic power source that came to their aid once before. Could it be relied upon to work again? he wondered. He pondered the idea that Marie suggested, that Tumalek himself might control this power source. Why was no one permitted to enter the deep cave where the prophet lived? How else would he have known that the Amakites were on the march? he questioned to himself.

The Harites employed no lookouts that far away. Still Gabriel had to have some faith in this unknown power because there was nothing else he could do. If the Amakites were not stopped, they could be upon the camp in less than two days.

A relatively small group of Harite warriors were picked to march out at first light to meet what might be the whole Amakite army on the Plain of Zofar. As Gabriel and Lemek walked back home, they talked about the preparations that they needed to make, and they talked about the prophecy of Tumalek. Since Lemek was a skilled artisan and weapons maker, he was never placed in a forward position in battle. He owned a fine sword that he made himself and was trained how to use it, but thus far in his life, he never had to.

Gabriel's mind contemplated his next move. He wrestled with three choices: First, he could find the doctor and Marie and flee in the shuttle to the safety of the *Odyssey*. Second, he could join the home guard and be trained how to fight with a sword. And third, he could observe and chronicle all that occurs and record it in a diary. Gabriel decided on the third option.

That night Gabriel collected and prepared the raw materials to make his diary. He gathered pieces of goatskins for paper. He then mixed together a primitive ink, which was more like paint. It was made from finely ground metal oxides in a light oil base. A pen was made from a small stick, partially hollowed in the center with the tip cut to a sharp angle.

Gabriel could not help looking at the cloud with an eerie luminance within it hovering over the camp. He knew that somewhere under that cloud, one thousand brave Harite warriors were preparing to march out in the morning to face an overwhelming enemy.

As the desert sky began to show some light even before the Cetian sun appeared, the blowing of hollowed-out animal horns could be heard on the north end of the camp. These horns had a very distinctive sound and were mostly used for the military. The brass horns were used for religious and general assembly purposes. A large group of soldiers and family members assembled just outside of camp.

The commander of the army was an older man named Eshtaol, who was appointed by the priests many years ago using a selection process that they claimed was specifically given by their god. It was Eshtaol who commanded the small Harite force on the mesa, engaging the Amakites in the battle that was observed by Gabriel and two other members of the expedition shortly after they arrived on this planet. Although Eshtaol was with his troops that morning, he was not to lead the regiment out to meet the enemy on the Plain of Zofar. Instead, that task was assigned to a younger officer named Kalem.

Kalem was a ruggedly handsome man who looked to be in his late thirties by Earth reckoning. He was married with five children. He stood out from most of his brethren in the great zeal that he projected toward the Harite god. But he was also a fierce and skilled warrior. And his men would always know to find him at the point of every engagement with the enemy. His shoulder-length golden-blond hair would protrude from around a hard leather helmet rimmed with a band of animal fur. He wore a simple leather breastplate and backplate over a soldier's tunic.

When the time came for the regiment to march, Kalem kissed his wife, who tried to show a quietly brave public face. He kissed his children, which made two of his youngest ones cry and cling to him as he tried to walk away. He knelt down and embraced his young children.

"Our god goes before us," he said with a confident smile.

Kalem got straight up and ran to the head of his troops. Other women and children did not suppress their feelings as cries and sobs could be heard throughout the crowd. Kalem pulled out his sword and pointed it straight up into the air, and then, with the same outstretched arm, he pointed the tip of the blade forward. With that, the regiment of Harite warriors marched out with the dark mysterious cloud moving ahead of them.

Robert Clarendon stood on the summit of a hill composed almost entirely of solid rock. From there, he could see his army behind him making their way through the various desert passes and onto the flat, dry Plain of Zofar. He could also see the northern Amakite divisions who had taken ships across the Sea of Ofir, marching in from the west. Clarendon checked in with his scouts through his communicator to determine if any Harite soldiers had been seen. At that point, no Harites could be seen. So the commander descended the hill to form his troops.

As evening approached, Clarendon ordered the Amakites to form a battle camp, which meant no tents and no fires. The king's army of more than twenty thousand men would sleep that night on the hard, sunbaked desert floor. If a man had to speak, he could only do so in soft whispers. Sentries were posted around the perimeter every ten paces and relieved every two hours. The more experienced Amakite officers told Clarendon that the Harites have been known to sneak up on their enemies at night, surround them, and attack quickly and fiercely while yelling and screaming wildly. They told him that the Harites did this to conceal their inferior force and to disorient the opponent. But Clarendon was determined that the forces he commanded would never be taken by surprise.

His forward scouts reported a strange spot of luminosity in the eastern sky. Clarendon could also see it from his position. At first, he reasoned that it was just a cloud backlit by the rising moon. He continued to observe this through the night and became disturbed to see that the cloud did not move nor did the luminosity within it ever diminish even though the moon had arched through the sky to be high above it. The commander did not share his apprehension with anyone. With only a few hours until dawn, he spread his bedroll over a flat rock and tried to get what sleep he could.

Kalem and his men had reached the open plain by the previous evening. They slept in the caves that surrounded the expansive plain. By dawn, the Harites formed two lines with each man standing about five paces from the other. On Kalem's orders, the regiment marched westward with the one dark grey cloud overhead moving ahead of them.

At last, word came to Clarendon over his communicator that a small Harite force could be seen approaching his position. Clarendon could see a single dark cloud over the far end of the plain, but he could not, at that time, see the Harites. He was still bothered by the presence of one low-hanging dark cloud in an otherwise clear and arid desert sky. Even the other members of the expedition, whatever their sympathies, believed that the Harites or someone working on their behalf must possess a technology that could control the weather. But Clarendon had superior force and momentum on his side, and he was not going to allow any doubts to derail his greater ambitions. From astride his horse in a rearward column, he gave the command to march forward.

It was early in the afternoon when the Amakites and Harites were close enough to see each other clearly. Both sides stopped their march when there was a distance of about half of a kilometer between the two forward lines. The dark cloud hovered low and ominously over the gap between them.

Clarendon removed his own handheld multiscanner from his pack. He switched it on and pointed it directly at the cloud. As data and wave patterns were lighting up the screen, he was getting some curious stares from the Amakites around him. He was looking for a concentration of some form of energy in or around the cloud. But when the scanner did not detect anything abnormal, he switched it off and put it away, barely hiding his frustration.

Most of the Amakite soldiers were becoming fearful of the dark and ominous cloud looming overhead. There could be heard some murmuring in the ranks, even among the officers. But each soldier remained in his position, fearing the terrible punishment for desertion or mutiny even more than the strange cloud, which seemed to be controlled by some unseen force. Sensing that his troops were losing their focus and resolve, Clarendon rode his large black stallion at a gallop to the front of the line.

He rode back and forth, shouting out to his troops, "Do not be afraid, it is only a cloud. It cannot harm you. Today we will have a complete victory. Do not fear the Harite magic, for we have far greater magic on our side."

With that, Clarendon pulled out his laser pistol and pointed it directly at the Harite front line. He squeezed the trigger, and with the sound of a short click and buzz, a lightning bright line of concentrated light flashed out and hit one of the Harite soldiers, causing him to yell out loudly, writhe in pain, and fall to the ground. Then with callous self-confidence, the commander again pointed his pistol at the Harite line. He hit another soldier, producing the same results.

The Amakites cheered as their confidence was renewed. The commander then holstered his weapon and returned to the rear of the column where the other high-ranking officers were stationed. When he arrived, he ordered the officers to advance and attack. But before the horns could sound, the cloud came down, covering the Amakite front lines in a thick, smoky fog where visibility did not exceed three meters.

The Amakite soldiers became disoriented. Their sense of direction was lost because they could not even see their own troops, much less the enemy. The ranks began to falter as talking increased from a few to many. The individual soldier was trying to stay with his unit while listening desperately for orders from officers that he could neither see nor hear. Finally, an order that was repeated and eventually was passed on over the sea of noise and confusion was heard.

"Be silent! Stand still!"

Nobody knew who the order originated with, but the common mind of these trained soldiers told them that it was the right thing to do, so they all complied. Soon the noise and confusion had ended. An eerie silence hung over the Amakites like the thick fog. Every soldier was standing still with his hands on his weapons, listening and watching intently in every direction.

After a few minutes of quiet tension, the frontline Amakites received a shocking surprise. Harite soldiers would suddenly appear out of the fog with a loud shout and swords swinging. The Harites would run up to the Amakite line and start hacking away with their swords as soon as an enemy soldier became visible. By the time the

Amakites realized who was approaching them, the Harites were upon them.

The Harites would deliver a death blow very quickly then immediately move to the next confused Amakite soldier. The chaos and the carnage became extreme. The Amakites assumed that they were being attacked by a much larger enemy force than was actually the case. So in their effort to strike before being struck down, the Amakites inadvertently killed and wounded many of their own men before they realized what they were doing.

The cloud covered only the front and middle lines of the Amakite infantry and left the rearward units and the high-ranking officers in the clear. The mounted lancers and the archers could not see the enemy, so they could not be brought into the battle. On the other side, the cloud ended just a few meters beyond the Amakite front line, which became decimated. The Harites were also in the clear, but they could run into the cloud and quickly find an enemy soldier to take down.

The Harites were divided into two lines of five hundred men. Kalem led the first attack. After about fifteen minutes of fierce fighting, they would withdraw from the cloud, and then the second line would run in. Clarendon could not see much more than the large, thick cloud in front of him. He could hear the yelling and the terrible sounds of battle, but he did not know what was happening. After this had gone on for almost an hour, even the commander became fearful. But he feared the loss of the king's army much more than he feared the cloud or the forces that controlled it.

Clarendon ordered the trumpeters to sound a retreat. The Amakites followed the sound of the trumpets and, with the help of their comrades, emerged out of the cloud and ran down the open plain overcome with great fear. The cloud followed the fleeing Amakites for a few kilometers then dissipated and vanished completely. The Harites stood on the Plain of Zofar solemnly watching with more than five thousand dead and dying Amakites at their feet.

CHAPTER 14

PURSUIT

Kalem stood before his troops. He took his sword in his right hand, holding the handle and hilt in the center of his chest with the blade pointed straight up in front of his face. The other Harite soldiers did the same. Then after a couple of seconds, Kalem swung the sword down and out to his side in a single rapid motion. His men followed his action in unison. This was the Harite warrior's salute to their god. It was a symbol of respect and thanksgiving.

The Harites suffered only five casualties in the battle. The two soldiers that took the laser hits suffered the worst; in fact, one of them had died. The other wounded soldiers were grazed by Amakite swords, but their wounds were recoverable. Kalem and most of his men were splattered with the blood of their enemies. Most of the soldiers wanted nothing more than to return to camp and their families. But as they started to turn back, Kalem stopped them.

Kalem told Joash, his second in command, to pick out ten soldiers to return to camp with their dead and wounded and to report back to the elders about the victory. But Joash protested. He thought that the entire regiment should return to camp. He believed that their mission was accomplished, at least for the time being.

"What are your intentions?" Joash demanded.

Kalem stood boldly and explained his plan to Joash and his men.

"The main force of the enemy army will separate and move south through the desert passes back toward Amakine. The smaller group will continue on the open plain to the Sea of Ofir, where they will take ships back home. We will follow their movements from far off, hiding in the hills that we know well. Then, before the enemy can take ship, while they are trapped against the sea, we will attack and destroy them."

Joash then argued back.

"The small force that you speak of is more than twice our strength!"

Kalem extended his arm out toward the desert ground where thousands of Amakite soldiers lay dead.

"Did our god not deliver much more than that into our hands this day?" Kalem asked rhetorically.

But Joash answered back, "The cloud of God is gone. We should not presume to know his will. We should go back and seek the advice of the elders or the prophet and be ready to defend our own people at home."

"This is not our home," Kalem replied sternly.

Then Kalem moved around to address the whole regiment.

"My brothers, I believe that we must give the enemy a reason to pursue us and not our women and children. With God's help, we must strike them down at every opportunity until they are driven from our land. But to this purpose, I want only those men who will put their whole heart in it. I will pursue the Amakites through the desert. All of those that agree with this will follow me. Those that do not agree will follow Joash back to defend the camp with all honor."

After that, the regiment divided itself almost equally in half with five hundred men gathered around Kalem and the others standing with Joash.

Joash was genuinely worried about Kalem and the men who would follow him. He feared that he would not see them again and that their people would lose five hundred of their best warriors. But Kalem placed great faith in the Harite god.

As the two groups prepared to move out in separate directions, Joash offered Kalem the Harite salute of respect. This was to place the right hand on the chest and bow the head down. The salute was not exclusively military, but it was used by any Harite toward a person of authority or any person deemed worthy of great respect. Kalem returned the salute. Joash gathered his troops along with the Harite dead and wounded and began their march back to camp. Kalem looked out over the vast expanse of desert and prepared his mind for a long march and a hard fight.

King Malcor was in Amakine with the anticipation of a great military victory in his campaign over the Harites. No reports had reached him, and the army was not expected to return for many days.

Meanwhile, the king was not just sitting idly on his throne. He sent Queen Lea out to all the cities of the valley to put a pleasing face on the brutal business of tax collection. Lea was more than happy with this assignment, for she was becoming addicted to the adoration of the common people. She was accompanied by a detachment of palace guards, several officers of the king, and a group of special enforcers, men who the queen had little knowledge of but who the wealthier Amakites knew well for their ruthless collection tactics.

The governors of each city were all summoned to the palace at Amakine. They were required to report directly to the king concerning all commerce within their districts and to pay their tribute.

Sandra Hirata did finally marry the young governor in a private ceremony in Jeku. But when the governors were later summoned to Amakine, the king requested that the governor of Jeku bring his new wife with him to the palace. As the governor and Sandra both stood before the king, he heaped praises and congratulations upon them.

Sandra wore a well-fitted red gown for her appearance in court. Her long jet-black hair hung down, pinned back on one side by a large gold hairpin. The king addressed most of his remarks to her husband, the governor, standing next to her. But Malcor's eyes would frequently glance back over to Sandra.

When questions and pleasantries were finished, Malcor did an unusual thing. He stood up as if to leave but stopped and bid the governor to speak with him privately in one of the anterooms. Sandra stood there alone for several minutes just being watched silently by some of the king's counselors up on the platform. She was becoming very concerned, for this was highly unusual. If the king meant to punish them, he would have issued a decree there and then.

Finally the governor came out alone and approached her with a melancholy look on his face. Sandra was getting worried. He came close to her and took her hand.

"You will stay here tonight," he said softly.

Sandra was curious and surprised.

"Why?" she asked.

"The king wishes it," he answered sadly.

When she realized what this meant, she simply stared down at the floor.

"It is considered a great honor," her husband said.

But Sandra angrily jerked her hand out of his and turned away from him. He touched her softly on the shoulder and told her that he would return for her at midmorning. As the young governor walked solemnly away from his wife, Tabar approached her gently.

"Do not be afraid, my lady. The king's desire is to give you great pleasure," he said.

Then Tabar escorted Sandra to the king's private residence.

Dr. Dunn and Marie Chenault had taken the shuttle back to the *Odyssey*. With the ship to themselves, they had spent many pleasant and intimate hours together. When the time came to discuss strategy, Dunn was trying to persuade Marie to join him in what amounted to mutiny against Commander Clarendon's authority. The doctor's rationale was that Clarendon had become mentally and emotionally unstable and that he was grossly interfering with the natural development of the indigenous culture. Marie was also becoming more convinced that this was the case.

All of the command and control computers on board recognized Robert Clarendon as the primary authority and Marie as the secondary. So Marie knew that she could not simply tell the computer that the commander was dead or lost since he could log in at any time through his communicator. But as the flight engineer, Marie had equal-access authority over navigation and the ship's engine systems.

Her plan was to start with her access to the navigation systems and then, step by step, link all of the other systems of the ship to those, thereby giving her equal command access to all of the ship's systems. Marie decided that the doctor should also have the same access in case of emergency.

After several hours of overriding standard protocols on the ship's computer to gain her access, she spent several more hours instructing the doctor on most of the other functions of the ship that he had not been trained in. The doctor was even shown how to scuttle the ship by decaying its orbit, which would be done only as an extreme last resort if the commander wanted to use it for some ill purpose. In such a case, the ship would be moved over a harmless location such as the open sea. The retro engines would begin a slow burn, which would give the occupants about four minutes to evacuate by shuttle before the ship began an irreversible fall.

But before Marie could finish her instructions on navigating the ship, a call came in over her communicator. The commander was ordering her to bring the shuttle down and land it five kilometers south of the Harite camp. The communicators could view detailed images of any area that was transmitted from space by the *Odyssey*.

Clarendon decided to use all of his technical assets to gain the military advantage. He could not detect any Harite troop movements. Kalem's soldiers were meandering their way through the rocky canyons south of the Plain of Zofar and were virtually undetectable from space. The commander could see the Harite camp in his view screen and the two streams of water that flowed through it. This satisfied his curiosity as to how the Harites sustained themselves in the desert. But to his surprise, he could detect no mobilization of troops within the camp.

The commander was not going to return a defeated army back to Amakine. He consulted with the other high-ranking officers, and they developed a plan of attack. The army would be split roughly in half. One force would move through the canyons and emerge out of the Plain of Zofar just north of the Harite camp. The other divisions would swing south through the desert to create a pincer move, surrounding the Harite camp on two sides.

Clarendon formed a reconnaissance group consisting of fifty fast-moving troops picked from the light infantry and archers. He personally gave these men a description of the shuttle craft with orders to guard it and let nobody approach it once they found it. He tore open a leather pouch and, with the tip of a knife, scratched out a rough drawing of the shuttle on the leather. Although his physical description of the shuttle was accurate, he told the soldiers that it was a war chariot with supernatural powers from the god Molak.

The shuttle craft had only two forms of access by the *Odyssey* crew—direct access and remote access. Direct access was any situation where crew members could board and pilot the shuttle directly, whether it was docked on the ship or on the ground. Remote access could only be acquired by Commander Clarendon or Marie Chenault. If the shuttle was unmanned, it could be ordered to or from any location by the ship's computer, and the ship's computer could be accessed by the communicators. But remote access would only work if the shuttle controls were set to autopilot. This was the default setting in which the shuttle was to operate and be left in. But over the last few weeks, Marie lost her trust in the commander. Since she could pilot the shuttle skillfully herself, she did not use the autopilot and left it turned off, thereby denying Clarendon remote access.

Neither Clarendon nor Marie would share with each other their doubts or suspicions; instead, they kept their communications brief with little or no explanation. Dr. Dunn tried to get Marie to ignore the commander's order. But she was not quite ready to start an open rebellion at that point. She relented. Marie and the doctor would take the shuttle down to a specified coordinate deep in the desert.

The morning after Clarendon sent his advance troops toward the Harite camp, he received a call over his communicator from one of his scouts in the hills. A few hundred Harite troops moving toward his position were seen in the canyons. As soon as the commander verified the strength of the Harite force, he devised a plan to outflank and trap them. He ordered the roughly two thousand troops from the northern valley and Ofir region to assemble in a narrow, open area by the sea. There they would take boats out to the fleet anchored out about one-third to one-half kilometer from the short beach. This was the location where these same troops landed several days before.

The commander knew that the embarkation process would take a few hours with the gusty winds and choppy waters in this part of the Sea of Ofir. This would be irresistible bait for the Harites to attack this vulnerable group with their backs to the sea. Meanwhile, the main force of the Amakite army would move farther back into the hills and let the Harites pass them. Then they would pivot left and emerge in the clearing behind the enemy force. The Harites would then be facing thirteen thousand Amakite troops surrounded by steep hills on both sides and with their backs to the sea.

The great open expanse of the Plain of Zofar narrowed considerably as one travelled westward toward the Sea of Ofir. A range of high, steep hills encroached upon the clearing, leaving it less than one-quarter of a kilometer wide by the seashore. Kalem and his troops had reached the summit of two hills after a long, hard climb. From there they could watch the choppy sea where the wind was producing whitecaps and one-meter swells. They could also see the fleet of ships and what looked to be two full regiments on the narrow beach struggling to board the small boats in the rough waters.

Most of Kalem's troops were crouched down or sitting on the back side of the hill so as not to be noticed by the enemy. Kalem was anxious to attack, but a young soldier sitting next to him who had no rank made a respectful suggestion.

"Sir, they are four times our number. If we attack now, our chance of victory will be small," the soldier said meekly.

"What do you propose?" Kalem asked scornfully.

The young soldier offered his advice, not knowing how it would be received.

"Let us wait until half of them are loaded onto the boats and well out to sea, then we attack the ones still on the beach. A good Harite soldier can kill at least two of the enemy in a fight, and those at sea cannot return in time to help them. And if they do return, we can kill them before they get out of the boats," the soldier concluded, waiting anxiously for a response.

Kalem thought for a moment.

"There is wisdom in your words. It shall be as you have said."

He smiled at the young soldier then issued an order for his men to wait for his signal to begin the attack.

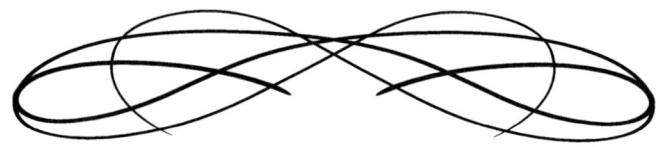

CHAPTER 15

BATTLE OF THE GODS

It was becoming late in the afternoon as Kalem and his small band of warriors watched the Amakites struggling to load their troops onto boats in the rough waters of the Sea of Ofir. Dark storm clouds had formed over the sea, which were not visible only an hour before. The cloud cover was spreading over the whole area. The wind and the waves were increasing in intensity. By the time that about half of the Amakites were either on the ships or in the boats, Kalem knew that it was the time to strike.

The fleet commanders saw that they had to depart quickly or risk foundering in the storm. They had stopped sending empty boats to the beach. Kalem stood up on the summit and raised his right arm straight up. He then swung it forward to signal the advance. The Harites descended the steep slopes in about fifteen minutes. But before they could reach the flat clearing below, they were spotted by almost one thousand Amakite soldiers still left on the beach.

The Amakites moved several meters farther away from the water's edge and quickly formed two defensive lines. The Harites had just begun to form up in the clearing. The formation they chose to use was called the Arrowhead. It was essentially a wedge or V pattern in which they would drive the point into the enemy center and concentrate their force on the thin edge of the enemy line where the two outside flanks could not be brought to bear quickly. Thereby a larger enemy force could be split in two.

When the arrowhead was formed, Kalem took the point. He raised his sword and turned back toward his troops. But before he could speak a word, he saw, to his horror, thousands of Amakite troops pouring out of the hills and forming up in the clearing not more than half a kilometer behind them. When Kalem's men saw the shocked look on his face, they all turned around to watch the bulk of the Amakite army forming up and preparing to attack. Once assembled, the Amakite army began to march forward.

Clarendon was up on a hillside with his field glasses, viewing from a vantage point where he could see all the troops on the plain. The Harites were trapped in a bottleneck with their backs to the sea. Kalem's demeanor had suddenly turned from confident warrior to a man vexed with guilt and sorrow. He sheathed his sword and began to speak personally to his men as emotion welled up inside him.

"My brothers, I beg for God's forgiveness and I beg for your forgiveness, for I alone have led you to your deaths. If I could die a death for each of you so that you might return to your families, I would happily do it. As for me, I am content to die with my brothers, fighting our enemy."

His soldiers stood silently for a moment until one of them yelled out, "We are brothers, and we are warriors! Whether it be life or death, let God be praised!"

Then the soldier gave the Harite warrior salute to their god. Following him almost in unison, the soldiers all shouted, "Let God be praised!"

Each one then gave the salute. Then Kalem, feeling whole and connected again to his comrades, shouted, "Let God be praised!" And he raised his sword in salute.

The wind gusts became stronger. Lightning strikes and thunder could be seen and heard in the hills all around the clearing. Then a torrential rain came, which fell at more than a forty-five-degree angle, driven by fierce winds coming off the sea. The few boats that had not yet made it back to the ships were being capsized by two-meter waves.

The ships were unable to maneuver in the strong head winds and high seas. The rain became more intense and intermittently mixed with ice, which was flying directly in the face of the Amakite army. The Amakites halted their advance. As the storm raged on, neither Harite nor Amakite were thinking about fighting as they watched nature erupt violently all around them.

The Sea of Ofir, being a large inland lake, was often known to have its own unique weather patterns. Sudden storms have been known to rise up without much warning, especially on the east side of the lake. Many boats were lost over the years in these dangerous waters, but storms of this magnitude have been rarely seen.

The wind increased even more as the cloud cover darkened from grey to black. One- and two-centimeter hail pelted the Amakite army so that they had to raise their shields in front of their faces or turn away completely. Then, to everyone's horror, a funnel cloud of high-intensity swirling winds touched down at sea directly over the fleet. Masts and oars were being snapped off the ships as many were being overturned by five-meter waves at the base of the whirlwind.

The funnel cloud increased in size and strength. Soon it became an enormous waterspout, pulling not only the water but anything in the water up into it. When water or solid objects reached the top of the funnel, they would be spewed out in all directions at high speeds, whatever their size or weight.

Down from the clouds began to fall boats and parts of boats. Even the dead bodies of men would drop in various places. The Amakites were becoming restless and fearful. When half of one of the trireme ships crashed to the ground in front of them, the Amakite lines began to falter, and panic spread through the ranks. When another almost-complete ship fell out of the dark clouds and smashed to pieces on the ground in the open clearing, fear completely took control over the Amakites. They ran as fast as they could back into the hills and canyons. It was every man for himself as some were trampled over by their comrades.

Many weapons were also left on the field in their haste to escape what they considered to be the wrath of a powerful god. Neither Clarendon nor any other officer could do a thing to stop the rout. Any orders they might give would never be heard over the wind and the rain.

Remaining on the beach were only a few hundred Amakites who had not been swept away by the waves. They dropped their weapons and ran to the Harites. When they reached Kalem's troops, the Amakites fell on their knees and bowed their heads to the ground in a gesture of complete surrender. Some of the Harites raised their swords against them, but Kalem stopped them. He told the Amakites to leave their weapons and go. The Amakite commander rose to his feet and bowed to Kalem. He then called his men together, and they also ran toward the hills to join their countrymen in retreat.

The whirlwind was weakening and eventually pulled back up into the clouds. In its wake was left a swirling and churning sea full of wreckage below. In a short time, the strong wind and heavy rains also diminished. The desert floor was strewn with a strange assortment of wreckage and debris. Even some fish could be seen scattered about still flapping around on the ground. In the midst of all this, the Harites stood alone in the clearing.

Clarendon stood his ground on the distant hillside, waiting to the last moment before following his army into the hills. He became frustrated by the ignorance and superstition of these primitive people but decided not to exact punishment on his men. He quickly realized that it was that very ignorance of science and technology that gave him his power over these people.

The commander knew that Earth had experienced even greater storms than that, so he certainly did not see it as being aberrant or supernatural. While slowly descending into the rugged canyon, his mind was busy devising his own divine wonders. Once again his plans had been thwarted. As he watched the enemy escape, in his mind he vowed that this would be the last time.

The use of communicators was, by prior agreement, to be kept to an absolute minimum. The view screens were all switched off for person-to-person communication. This, of course, was done to avoid frightening or confusing a technologically primitive people. Marie was giving Clarendon one last benefit of the doubt that he may have reconsidered becoming further entangled with native conflicts. The doctor, however, had less faith in the probability of Clarendon coming to his senses.

After about an hour of waiting and walking around the shuttle scanning the desert, Marie and the doctor decided to pack some equipment and make the two-hour hike to the Harite camp. Once again, the doctor strapped on the holster that contained the flare pistol. The shuttle was sealed securely. If Clarendon arrived while they were gone, he could access the shuttle by using the entry keypad next to the hatch. But Marie left the autopilot off, so he still could not access it remotely. She and the doctor made an agreement that they would give the commander forty-eight hours.

Gabriel was gradually becoming more prominent in Harite society. Because he was a stranger who was willing to live among them and because he seemed intelligent and inventive, he drew the interest and favor of many Harites. On more than one occasion, it was made known to him, in not so subtle terms, by prominent families that their daughter would make an excellent wife. But the satisfying of desires would indeed be not as simple or immediate as it had been on Earth. Gabriel decided to defer any such commitment but also realized that he could not do so indefinitely.

He continued to work with Lemek on his improved forge. Most of the work in the past few weeks had been for swords and other weapons. Miram and Yakob would sometimes stop by to see them, which always made Gabriel happy. But on that day, Gabriel would welcome two other friends. He saw the doctor and Marie walk into camp. They were not hard to spot with their blue jumpsuits and shiny aluminum backpacks. He dropped his work and ran over to greet his shipmates.

The camp was much busier and more agitated than normal. Since the return of Joash and his men, people could be seen running about the camp, spreading the news about their victory at Zofar. But concerning Kalem and his five hundred men, there was still no word, which had many families worried.

Marie and Dr. Dunn by this time were also well-known in the camp. Before long, a Harite man approached the doctor and indicated that he wanted him to see something several meters away in the distance. Gabriel followed and served as translator.

The doctor, Marie, and Gabriel followed the man to the outskirts of camp to an improvised Harite cemetery where the ground was soft enough to dig. There they saw two bodies covered with white linen sheets lying on the ground near two open graves recently dug for them. The man knelt down and removed the sheets. They both were Harite soldiers killed in the recent battle. The Harite pointed to the strange burn wounds on both soldiers. The families and many others were curious about what killed them since it was reported that no enemy soldier got near enough to them to strike a blow.

Several Harites gathered around, but they stood back and mostly kept silent after explaining that the man on the left died in the battle and the other man died from his wounds some time later. Dr. Dunn walked over to the body of the soldier who died most recently. Flanked by Marie and Gabriel, the doctor cut the burned tunic over the wound.

"Oh god," Gabriel gasped and then turned away.

Marie remained silent, simply closing her eyes for a couple of seconds, and then opened them again slowly.

"It's all right, Gabriel. It can't hurt you," the doctor scoffed at Gabriel's squeamishness. "Look at this."

"This is very strange," he continued.

"It isn't just a cut or stab wound. The tissue and blood vessels have been seared closed," the doctor explained.

Gabriel was puzzled.

"What could have done that?" he asked.

"He was cut and burned at the same time," the doctor answered.

"A red-hot piece of metal?" Gabriel offered a speculation in search for an answer.

The doctor pondered for a moment.

"Or a laser blast," the doctor muttered.

Gabriel was surprised.

"Do you think that the Amakites got hold of the commander's laser pistol and learned how to use it?" he asked.

"Not the Amakites, the commander," the doctor answered without reservation.

"That's hard to believe," Gabriel answered back.

Dr. Dunn turned to Gabriel.

"You've been away for a long time. Our illustrious commander now fancies himself to be the Julius Caesar of this planet," the doctor explained.

Gabriel began to put it all together in his mind, realizing that what the doctor was saying could be all too probable. Then Gabriel spoke out his thoughts openly.

"Imagine a Julius Caesar with access to advanced technology," he postulated.

The doctor looked over to Marie. He covered the body and stood up.

"We've got to go!" he said urgently.

"Go where?" Gabriel asked.

"Come on, Jim!" Marie yelled then slipped her backpack on and started running.

Dr. Dunn looked back at Gabriel.

"Take care of yourself, Gabriel," he said and then quickly turned and ran after Marie.

Gabriel felt very uneasy letting the Harites see his friends run away and leave him to answer their questions. He wondered, how does anyone explain a high-intensity laser weapon and its effect on human flesh to a native of this planet? This time, he uncharacteristically decided to play ignorant.

With Marie still in the lead, she and the doctor continued their run past several bewildered Harites out to the sparse outskirts of the encampment then into the open desert. The doctor soon became winded and had to stop for a couple of minutes. Marie looked back and stopped herself. They decided to continue at a modest jog, travelling a bit slower but stopping less often. The hills and rock formations were still fresh in their minds from when they passed them earlier that day. Finally, after a long, hot trek through the desert, they were relieved to see the shuttle craft in the distant clearing where they had left it.

The star Tau Ceti hung low in the sky as the late-afternoon shadows grew longer. Marie and the doctor were walking together while keeping the shuttle in sight, which at that point was only about one-quarter of a kilometer away. But the doctor sensed some movement up in the hills. Again he saw a figure move on the summit of a nearby hill. He stopped to take a better look.

"What is it?" Marie inquired as she stopped with the doctor.

"I thought I saw something or someone moving around up there," the doctor said softly.

Marie looked up at the low, rocky hills, which were mostly in shadow.

"I don't see—"

Marie stopped speaking as she saw the figures of four or five men on a hilltop silhouetted against a still lighted sky. After that, they immediately began seeing more men on the other hills; some were moving down the slopes in their direction. These men were dressed as soldiers carrying swords and other weapons. The doctor took off his backpack and laid it on the ground.

"Take your backpack off, quick!" the doctor said anxiously.

He grabbed Marie's backpack and helped her off with it.

"We've got to make a run for it. Go!" he commanded.

As soon as they started running, they drew the attention of the soldiers coming out of the hills. There was immediate shouting among the soldiers, who tried to hasten their decent down the rocky slopes to the clearing where the shuttle rested. Some of them slid and fell on the loose rocks and gravel. Marie and the doctor continued to run with all that was in them. They had only about one hundred meters to go.

The doctor heard an arrow whiz over his head but did not turn to look where it came from; he just kept running forward with his eyes on the shuttle. Another arrow skidded along the ground just behind them. The shuttle was only a few meters away from Marie and the doctor as some of the soldiers reached the clearing. Marie lunged for the keypad as another arrow bounced off the shuttle. When she completed the code, the outer hatch began to slowly open. They were both prepared to run into the airlock even before the hatch opened completely.

Then Marie let out a loud scream. The doctor looked at her and saw, to his horror, an arrow sticking out of her back. He looked back and saw the archer gaining on them. The soldier stopped momentarily to prepare another shot. Almost without thinking, the doctor pulled out his flare pistol, aimed it at the archer, and fired. The white-hot flare hit the soldier in midtorso, which then caused his entire body to burst into flames. The soldier screamed and flailed about for a few seconds before falling to the ground dead, his body still burning. This slowed the advance of most of the others. Then almost out of nowhere, another soldier was running wildly up to the doctor, yelling with an upraised sword in his hand. The doctor took quick aim at the soldier's head. The flare entered the soldier's open mouth and blew his head apart in a horrific flaming blast. All of the soldiers stopped in their tracks and then backed away in a slow retreat. Though they were fierce warriors under strict orders, they believed that gods who can throw balls of fire and burst men into flames should not be tampered with.

Marie was lying on the deck of the shuttle, facedown with her legs still hanging outside. The bloodstain on her jumpsuit was growing around the wound. The doctor carefully lifted her up and pulled her inside. He laid her in the narrow walkway between the seats and the bulkhead. He then closed the hatch. Marie was bleeding heavily from the back, and she was starting to cough up blood because the arrow had punctured her right lung. The doctor's main concerns were to immediately slow the external bleeding then to get her into the operating room aboard the *Odyssey* as soon as possible. He rushed to the medical compartment and grabbed several compresses and tape. He pressed the compresses around the arrow shaft and taped them down to her jumpsuit. Unfortunately, the shears that he needed to cut through the jumpsuit were back on the *Odyssey*.

He looked toward the control panel, frustrated and angry at himself that he had never learned the launch procedures. He went over to Marie and gently lifted her head up.

"Marie, tell me what to do," he gently asked.

Marie started to speak but coughed up more blood. She tried again, but she was getting weaker and struggling to breathe.

"Switch on navigation computer." She struggled, interrupted by coughing and hard breathing.

"Power on engines." She gasped in great distress.

"Switch to autopilot." She spoke not much above a whisper.

"Select home." These were her last words before losing consciousness.

The doctor performed the sequence as Marie told him. The computer then asked him if he wanted to select the three-minute countdown.

"No, damn it, launch immediately!" the doctor answered angrily.

The hydrogen engines started to roar, and the doctor, who was leaning forward over the console, was thrown back into the pilot seat as the shuttle lifted off quickly.

The Amakite soldiers watched in amazement and reverence as the great war chariot returned to the gods.

The doctor had propped up Marie's head with a floatation device and placed an oxygen mask on her face while trying to keep her as still as possible during the flight. Marie struggled through the twenty-minute flight and docking procedure. Finally, the light turned green over the hatch, and the doctor opened it. He carried Marie through the airlock and into the assembly area. Without regard to the pain developing in his arms, he carried her facedown, keeping her back as free from flexing as possible. They moved down the service corridor and into the operating room. Marie was laid down on her stomach with her face in a form-fitting headrest where she could receive oxygen.

The doctor walked into the airtight sanitary surgery suit from which he could control all aspects of the operation by speaking to and listening to the computer from inside the glass helmet. Immediately the doctor activated the computer by speaking in the helmet. He gave the computer the patient's name and title as well as a concise description of the injury. The operating room had the whole blood, stem cells, and the complete medical history of each crew member. The operating room contained every instrument, drug, and anesthetic that a surgeon would need. Precision robot arms were at the doctor's command. They could perform all of the needed functions better than a room full of assistants.

After the doctor cut away the top part of Marie's jumpsuit, the overhead module immediately began to install monitors and inject intravenous lines. The computer not only monitored but could diagnose and recommend procedures. But in this department of the ship, Dr. Dunn was the absolute master.

Commander Clarendon had gathered back the bulk of his scattered army. They were on the last leg of their march back to Amakine. Campfires, tents, and makeshift lean-tos filled one wide canyon from one end to the other.

That night the commander paced back and forth, lost in strategic thoughts. At one point, he sat down and thought to pull out his communicator. He logged onto the ship's computer to check the shuttle location and status. He saw that it was subject to remote access. Somebody had left the autopilot switched on. Clarendon jumped up and ran to the nearest clearing large enough for the shuttle to land in. He ordered the ship's computer to pilot the shuttle to those coordinates immediately.

Clarendon had long ago given up the idea of hiding technology from these people. Instead, he would exploit it for all of the advantage and influence it could give him. That night, his whole army was to witness a glowing, pulsing war chariot descend from the sky, summoned down to their world by their commander, who, they would come to believe, had direct access to the gods.

CHAPTER 16
THE TURNING POINT

The following morning was a cause for celebration in the Harite camp as Kalem and his troops returned without a man lost. While soldiers returned to their families, Gabriel decided to visit Miram on the pretext of spreading the good news. Miram also had the same idea, and they met up with each other about halfway between, next to the stream. They began to speak at the same time, telling each other the news that they already knew. They laughed and then looked with desire upon each other. Gabriel was not only physically attracted to Miram but he felt comfortable and at home around her. He always liked Miram very much, but now he felt those feelings developing into something much stronger. Gabriel could hold back no longer. He walked up to Miram, put his arms around her, held her close, and kissed her passionately. She responded with all her body and feelings, momentarily not caring what any passerby might think. When they separated, their eyes spoke of how much they wanted each other.

But a commotion was stirring in the camp. Runners were shouting something. Gabriel and Miram turned their attention to what was going on around them. At last they heard and understood what was being said.

"Tumalek is dead! Tumalek is dead!"

Apparently the old prophet had just died. The Harites were sad and unsettled by this. They had known him for many years. He gave them guidance at critical times and, on occasion, delivered messages to the people that, they believed, came directly from their god.

Miram had known him as a prophet all of her life. She was visibly distressed by the news, so Gabriel took her hand and started to walk her home along the stream. As he looked at the water in the stream, Gabriel noticed that the volume was much lower. It was almost half of what it was just the day before. Miram noticed it also. Soon the whole camp would be stirred up by another crisis. The flow of water in the stream, which had not varied for a hundred years, was at that time rapidly diminishing.

Based on the prophecy, the Harites knew that this time would come soon. So they kept their jugs and jars filled, as well as animal-skin canteens and community barrels. Every Harite took this opportunity to top off their water supply. When this was done, the steady stream of water that had sustained them for a century had completely stopped.

The trumpets sounded throughout the camp. Soldiers gathered their weapons and battle gear. They would assemble with their units, and the army would lead the people westward toward the river valley. Families began pulling up tent stakes and loading everything that was portable onto pack animals. The Harites had few carts due to the scarcity of wood in the desert. So every man, woman, and child above age ten or so had their burden to bear.

The Harite people were never truly nomadic, as many other people had assumed. Since the early days of their forced exile, the Harites would occasionally raid the villages of the valley for grain, seed, and animals. Soldiers would engage in remote skirmishes with their Amakite enemies. But they would always return to their camp. The Harites would leave behind some permanent stone structures, many productive gardens, and their dead, all to be reclaimed inevitably by the desert.

Dr. Dunn stood motionless after Marie's vital signs had flatlined on the monitors sometime in the early morning hours. The surgery to remove the arrow and repair the damaged tissues was long, but the doctor accomplished it skillfully. However, the trauma to the internal organs and loss of blood were too much for Marie to recover from. The doctor stayed with her to the end. He slowly stepped out of the sanitary suit. As he covered Marie's body, his eyes welled up with tears, which he tried to hold back but could not. He could not bring himself to move her to the cold storage room at that time, so he walked around the ship trying to cope with his loss. He still did not realize that the shuttle had been taken by remote during the night and that, for the time being, he was marooned on the ship.

Clarendon examined the shuttle alone while his soldiers had strict orders not to approach within twenty paces. He noticed the bloodstains on the deck but did not ponder over them for long. He disengaged the autopilot and set about looking for anything he could use to gain a military advantage. The commander fixed his gaze on the thick metal hatch marked Danger Explosive Fuel, which was in the middle of the rear bulkhead. The hatch itself was only one and a half meters tall.

Clarendon moved to the back of the shuttle, stooped down, and opened the hatch. This was the fuel storage compartment for the shuttle's engines. The compartment held two carbon fiber cylinders just under one meter in height by about thirty centimeters in diameter. The cylinders contained highly compressed hydrogen gas. They were locked automatically onto one-way valves that connected directly to the engine fuel lines. One tank could fuel more than three hours of flight.

The commander closed the hatch and ran to the flight computer at the pilot's console. Tank number 1 was down 42 percent. Tank number 2 was still at 100 percent full. He knew that the small maneuvering engines on the *Odyssey* used hydrogen as well. He also knew that the ship carried several of these small tanks that could be refilled by the ship's main tank. As he pondered the potential power that he had at his command, a devious smile emerged on his face.

"Now I have the stronger magic," he said to himself.

The Amakite army marched in unit formation through the river valley. It did not look like an army in retreat, but proud and triumphant as it approached the gates of Amakine. The watchmen on the wall saw them from a distance and heralded their coming. When it appeared that the whole army was in the flatlands, the watchmen and officials who went up on the wall to look were somewhat curious at the procession.

The army seemed somewhat diminished. Trumpets sounded a victory march, but no enemy captives could be seen. Then from just over the hilltops, the shuttle craft flew low over the army also heading directly toward the city. The gates were open, and the army began to march in.

The shuttle moved very slowly and flew right over the wall, as if to lead the army into the city. The people of the city were spellbound. Many were yelling and screaming to their families and neighbors to come see the wondrous sight. Clarendon had received the reaction he hoped for. He would have the attention of everyone, even the king, and convince them all that their gods were more powerful than all of their enemies.

The commander stood before King Malcor, Queen Lea, and all of the royal council to report on the expedition. He did admit to a temporary setback in their campaign to subdue the Harites. He argued his case before the king very forcefully and logically. This was to be one of the few occasions that he would explain something to the king that he actually believed to be true himself.

He went on to explain, "The eastern desert is known to have dramatic changes in temperature and a great variety of land formations. This makes it subject to sudden and extreme weather patterns. Your Majesty will remember that before I arrived, hundreds of troops were lost in a violent storm."

The king nodded. Clarendon continued to explain.

"I believe that over many years, the Harites have learned to forecast these storms and recently applied that knowledge for military advantage." He paused a moment, waiting for the king's reaction.

The king seemed fascinated by the theory but had no questions at the moment. Lea glared at Clarendon skeptically but held her peace. Clarendon continued.

"In every encounter, the Harites have chosen the time and place of battle. When the clouds or storms come, our soldiers believe that the Harite god is more powerful, but it is not true."

Clarendon stopped as the king interrupted.

"How do you plan to overcome this?" the king asked.

Clarendon stood confidently and answered, "I asked the gods of the Amakites for help, and they answered me. They sent me a war chariot that I alone can drive. They also have sent weapons of fire and thunder that will make all of your enemies tremble with fear. I propose another expedition, but this time we will attack suddenly and without warning, using our heavenly weapons. This time, I will choose the time and place of battle, and we will have victory."

The commander concluded his remarks with almost a patriotic fervor.

The king rose to his feet with renewed ambition. He spoke to address not only Clarendon but the entire court.

"You will have all of the troops you need. I will summon the reserves from all of the other cities and villages here to Amakine. Civilians in the city will give up their homes to the troops until they are ready to march. They all shall be at your command. And let us thank and honor the gods."

After the king spoke, everyone bowed, and the king left the court followed by his councilors.

Lea was left seated on the platform next to the king's throne. She rose, walked over to Clarendon, and spoke softly but authoritatively.

"I hope you know what you're doing. We didn't bring any weapons except for your laser pistol," she said with a condescending tone.

"Your Highness would do well to leave such things to me," Clarendon replied in a sarcastic tone mocking her title.

"I am your queen, General," Lea answered back in a tone mocking his title.

Clarendon inwardly fumed but then quickly composed himself to respond.

"Is Your Highness aware of what happens when one ignites highly compressed hydrogen gas?" he asked her as if she were in elementary school.

Lea was curious.

"What?" she asked.

"An explosion the likes of which this planet has never seen. The enemy will believe that hell itself has broken out. The ones that are not killed by the blast will quickly surrender," he answered.

Lea nodded.

"We are pleased to hear it," she said.

Clarendon turned around and walked away without another word.

CHAPTER 17
A FIRE IN THE SKY

The next morning was filled with activity in Amakine as soldiers were sporadically coming into the city from all other parts of the valley. Civilians in the city were leaving their homes by the king's decree and lodging with people in the other cities and the countryside to give billeting to the thousands of soldiers being assembled for the next invasion.

Amakine was becoming an armed camp. Still many people paused to get a look at the strange war chariot resting in the middle of one of the widest streets near the central square. The shuttle craft was completely encircled by guards armed with lances and swords. They stood almost shoulder to shoulder with their backs to the shuttle and facing the crowd. But no curious spectator dared to approach closer than ten paces to these very serious guards.

Shouts could be heard from the back of the crowd as a detachment of soldiers was making its way through. Civilians moved aside or were pushed away by some forty armed soldiers marching in two columns moving directly toward the shuttle. Clarendon and two other officers were in the middle. The detachment stopped by the guards, who opened up a gap for Clarendon to go in. Everyone else waited outside the circle.

Clarendon accessed the keypad, opened the hatch, and walked inside. He quickly closed the hatch behind him. Much talking and murmuring could be heard from the crowd outside. He went to the pilot's console, activated the computer, and sent a command to the fuel compartment to disengage tank number 2. Then Clarendon moved to the fuel compartment, opened the hatch, and carefully removed the hydrogen cylinder.

Although Clarendon thought through the process of converting fuel tanks into weapons, he felt that he needed to put his theory to the test. He had the cylinder placed on the sparsely grassy ground about fifty meters outside the western wall. The whole area was cleared of any people from the wall to the river.

Only a few officers and soldiers to render assistance were permitted on that part of the wall to witness the commander's experiment. The Amakites followed orders, but they had no idea what was about to happen. Clarendon was hedging his bet by testing his theory with few witnesses just in case the results were not as spectacular as he had hoped.

Clarendon was dressed in the full tunic, robe, and ornate armor of his rank as he walked up the steps to the top of the wall and over to the outer parapet. He looked over and saw the cylinder on the ground below. His officers were looking at him, awaiting further orders or wondering what would happen next. Without a word, he pulled his laser pistol out of the holster and switched the power on. The small gauge on the weapon indicated that the power pack was getting low. That meant that he only had three or four blasts left at full power. Clarendon took careful aim at the cylinder and squeezed the trigger. A short, bright laser blast scorched the grass just a few centimeters next to the cylinder.

He looked again at the gauge showing the power pack depleted a little more. For his second shot, he rested his hand on the solid stone block. He took a few more seconds to aim then squeezed the trigger. A deafening boom was heard, and the next thing he saw was a giant wall of flame all in front of him. Clarendon quickly fell back behind the parapet as did several others. Some dropped to the deck as soon as they heard the explosion. And a few who were leaning over to get a better look were burned by the fast-rising flames. A huge fireball that could be seen by the entire city rose high into the sky then vanished in a rising plume of dark smoke.

Clarendon rose to his feet and stood back until the thickest of the smoke dissipated. Much yelling and some panic could be heard in the city. Clarendon walked over to the inside part of the wall where he could be seen. In a very theatrical gesture, he stood over the crowd with his arms extended out and smoke still rising up behind him. All of the soldiers began to cheer.

The Harite people were moving slowly through the barren desert. Experienced soldiers who had travelled through those regions before were finding the best trails and leading the way. Most of the women and children along with the elderly never travelled very far from camp. So the rough terrain became a struggle for many. The elders assigned men not designated as soldiers to assist anyone who needed help to keep moving their families and goods along. Gabriel was one of those men. He spent most of his time walking with Miram and Yakob but occasionally helped neighboring families as needed. One family who had several small children was having difficulty negotiating the rocks and crevasses of a long dry wash. So Gabriel lifted their little girl onto his shoulders and carried her over two kilometers. Hope was mixed with anxiety for the vast Harite tribe, which was scattered over several square kilometers of desert. Many had hoped to see the cloud of God, but it was nowhere to be seen.

Sandra Hirata was safe in her large home in Jeku. But after her liaison with the king, she underwent a change in her normal upbeat outlook and demeanor. She stayed in the house more often and occasionally succumbed to bouts of depression. At that point, she was having mixed feelings about her husband the governor. She told him that she would never set foot in the city of Amakine again, even if her husband had to go there. Since then, she had not spoken anymore about her ideas concerning public health and sanitation. She had come to believe that the whole society was, at its core, barbaric.

But the valley was active, including the city of Jeku, with the influx of people and families from Amakine seeking temporary housing. Even the governor's large home was not exempt from the requirement to give shelter to the displaced families. Unlike most of the Amakites who complied grudgingly with the king's order, Sandra began to take some humanitarian pride in offering her home and food to several of those needy families.

Clarendon sent word to King Malcor that in two days, at midday, he would enter the chariot and ascend to the gods. He would then return in a short time with instructions and weapons to subdue all of the king's enemies. The commander would need every bit of that time to set up duty schedules and to ensure that order would be maintained in a city full of restless men. The king made this task more difficult by ordering celebrations and sacrifices to the various Amakite gods.

Prostitutes remained in Amakine, and many were brought in from other cities to freely ply their trade in the private homes of the families who were sent away. Publicly sponsored prostitutes were also active in the temples built for each deity. Clarendon felt that he had to separate himself from baser activities, at least as long as his troops and the king saw him as a messenger of the gods. He reasoned that for a little strategic restraint applied now that the future would hold unlimited possibilities for him. The commander planned to return to the *Odyssey*, where there were two extra power packs for the laser and at least a dozen empty fuel cylinders that he could fill with compressed hydrogen. Between the arsenal he could assemble and his knowledge of Harite tactics, Clarendon truly believed that victory was already his.

As Kalem's unit rounded the hill into one of the many canyons in that part of the desert, he and his men were very surprised by what they saw. There were about fifty Amakite soldiers just standing there at the bottom of the canyon. They appeared worn-out, hungry, and thirsty. As Kalem and his men approached, the Amakites did not move or seem afraid. They lacked the will or the means to put up a fight since most of them were unarmed. Still, Kalem signaled to his troops entering the canyon to surround the Amakites. The Harites approached them with swords drawn. The Amakite soldiers stood still and watched almost with anticipation as the Harites came closer. Then the commander of the small Amakite band walked directly toward Kalem. The Amakite seemed familiar to him. He moved slowly and carried no weapon while keeping his hands open and visible.

The Amakite officer stopped and fell to his knees just a few meters in front of Kalem and bowed down to him. When the other Amakites saw this, they also bowed down to Kalem and the Harite soldiers. Kalem ordered the officer to rise and speak. When the Amakite stood up and looked him in the eye, Kalem recognized him as the officer in charge of the Amakite regiment on the shore of the Sea of Ofir. Kalem received his surrender at that time, and he let the survivors go. But Kalem was very curious as to why these men were not back in their country. The Amakite began to speak.

"We are your prisoners. We know that you serve a powerful god. No army and no country can stand against him. He will give your people all of the river valley and all of the cities and towns in it and all of the people in it. Please spare the lives of my men and our families, and we will serve you and your god for the rest of our lives."

Kalem sheathed his sword and looked with compassion on his former enemy.

"Only those who resist us will be put to the sword. All others will be spared," he told the Amakite.

Kalem offered the Amakite a drink from his own waterskin. He then ordered that the Amakites be taken to Eshtaol with Kalem's recommendation that those Amakites be made a special unit in the Harite army to supply intelligence on Amakite fortifications and troop strength in the valley. If the aging commander agreed and the Amakites proved themselves, they would be given positions of trust and honor in the Harite army. The forward units were scheduled to reach the summits of the hills overlooking the river valley by about midday on the following day.

The time came when Supreme Commander Robert Clarendon was to enter the war chariot and ascend to the gods. The entire city turned out to watch. King Malcor and Queen Lea had commandeered an entire building with a large balcony that overlooked the central square. Their purpose was not only to get the best view in the city but also to be seen by as many of the people as possible.

The crowd became suddenly quiet as Clarendon opened the outer hatch and walked inside. After the hatch closed, the crowd waited silently for about five minutes until the bright red and yellow warning lights started flashing on and off around the shuttle. About a minute later, the engines fired up with an increasing roar. The guards and many of the people standing nearby could feel the hot thrust blow past them. The shuttle lifted up off the street, slowly at first, and then as it rose higher above the city, it accelerated its rate of climb. When the shuttle finally disappeared into the sky, the whole city cheered, and soon began an orgy of celebration.

Dr. Dunn spent most of his time exploring various areas of the ship and the computer systems with which he had the least amount of training. Still he spent many hours sitting, thinking, and remembering. When that became too painful, he would sleep for long periods with the aid of sedatives.

The doctor was sleeping in his cabin when Clarendon brought the shuttle craft home to dock with the *Odyssey*. The distant clang of the docking arms engaging or the hiss of the air seals opening did not wake the doctor even though the door of his cabin was wide open.

Clarendon came out of the airlock and immediately saw that the staging area was empty. But he did notice several drips of dried blood on the deck. He walked up to the bridge, expecting to see Marie or the doctor and perhaps even Gabriel. But the bridge was also empty. He moved down the central corridor and noticed the door open in Dr. Dunn's cabin. Clarendon peeked in quietly and saw the doctor sleeping. He decided not to wake him and that it would be best for him not to have to explain to anyone what he was doing.

Clarendon proceeded as quickly and quietly as he could. He stopped at Marie's cabin, which was closed. He gently opened the door but found it to be empty. The next stop was his own cabin, where he went directly to a locked cabinet that contained two power packs for his laser. He immediately replaced the spent power pack with a fully charged one and put the spare in a holster pouch. Then he moved quickly to the back end of the corridor where the engine room was located. He used the palm ID scanner to open the hatch.

The engine room was quiet at that time with no engines active. He saw twelve empty fuel cylinders secured in racks near the large hydrogen fuel tank that powered the ship's maneuvering engines. Filling the cylinders was fully automated, taking only a few seconds per cylinder. Clarendon could carry two cylinders at a time, but they were cumbersome and a bit slippery when held by just one arm. He managed to deliver six full cylinders to the shuttle staging area, which was no short distance from the engine room. It amounted to traversing more than half of the total length of the ship with each trip.

On his next trip, he stumbled just outside of the corridor. One of the cylinders he was carrying dropped on the deck, rolled, and knocked against the bulkhead. The noise woke the doctor. He opened his eyes and sat up. Clarendon scrambled to pick up the cylinder and moved them quickly to the staging area. The doctor stood up and followed the sound of the noise. He confronted Clarendon as he was standing with the two cylinders next to the others.

"What are you doing?" the doctor demanded.

Clarendon acted surprised.

"Jim, I'm sorry. I didn't mean to wake you," Clarendon responded with feigned concern.

"What are those for?" the doctor asked, referring to the cylinders.

"These are fuel cylinders for the TLV. I was planning an extended reconnaissance of the various inhabitants on this part of the planet," Clarendon replied in a cool and calculating manner.

"Reconnaissance?" the doctor questioned.

"Exploration, you know what I mean, the reason why we all came here. I was about to discuss my plans with Marie. By the way, where is she?" Clarendon responded with increasing impatience.

"She's dead," the doctor answered flatly.

"Dead? How? When?" Clarendon seemed genuinely surprised.

"She was shot with an arrow. I operated on her. She held on for a few hours, but the internal damage and loss of blood were too much. Her body just shut down," the doctor explained as he felt all the emotions of his loss come back in full as he recounted the incident to the commander.

"I'm sorry, Jim. You did everything you could. She was a good officer," Clarendon said in a conciliatory tone.

"Yes, she was a good officer, perhaps too good," the doctor retorted as his sadness was quickly turning into anger.

"What are you talking about?" Clarendon asked.

"She was too good of an officer to disobey your orders even though we were led into a trap!" the doctor said as the volume and tone of his voice was becoming increasingly hostile.

"What in hell are you talking about? You can't think that I knew anything about this," Clarendon responded almost as forcefully.

"It was an Amakite arrow, Commander. Amakite soldiers, Commander. Your little chums just waiting for us, hiding in the hills," the doctor argued as his anger and volume intensified.

"Look, Jim, these people have been at war with each other for years. They send raiding parties back and forth all the time. Unfortunately, you and Marie happened to run into one. Now I feel terrible about what happened to Marie, but I had nothing to do with it," the commander explained while trying to act reasonable.

"They just happened to be there, out in the middle of nowhere, a hundred kilometers from home at the same time and in the same place that you ordered Marie to land the shuttle," the doctor countered the commander by posing his explanation in such a way as to make it seem logically absurd.

"How can I know where every Amakite is or what they are doing at all times?" the commander rebutted.

"You're their glorious leader, the king's trusted general. Just look at yourself. It's over. It ends now," the doctor said. After which he began to move toward Clarendon.

But the commander drew his laser sidearm and aimed it directly at the doctor.

"Stop right there," the commander said sharply.

The doctor stopped in his tracks.

"Now you go back to your cabin, Doctor. I'll be back in a few days. In the meantime, try to come to your senses," the commander told the doctor in an authoritarian tone.

Dr. Dunn stood still, looking the commander in the eye for a few seconds. Then he slowly began to back up and walked back to his cabin. When the doctor was out of sight, Clarendon holstered his sidearm and started loading the cylinders onto the shuttle. The doctor closed the door of his cabin and went over to activate the computer terminal at his desk. He pulled up the visual feed from the staging area camera. As he watched the commander's movements on his monitor, a desperate resolution filled his mind.

It took the commander about ten minutes to load the cylinders and everything else that he intended to take with him on the shuttle. He then entered the airlock and closed the hatch. When the doctor saw this, he leaped out of his seat and ran out of his cabin toward the bridge.

The doctor logged onto the ship's command and control computer as Marie had instructed him. He knew that he might only have about a minute before the commander switched on the shuttle computer. Doing so would establish an unbreakable link of control between the shuttle and the ship.

Clarendon had to spend a few minutes securing the loose hydrogen cylinders in the seats with the safety harnesses. There was no facility on board to store such cargo. After the cylinders were secured for the trip, the commander went to the pilot's console. Dr. Dunn had successfully circumvented the normal protocols and issued emergency procedure orders to the computer. First he commanded that the airlock hatches and the docking arms be locked in the closed position. When Clarendon heard the clang of the solenoid-activated bolts engage, he stopped for a second, thinking something was wrong. He reached over to switch on the navigation computer. But before he could, the console and the whole interior of the shuttle went dark.

The doctor had shut down all power and computer linkage from the ship to the shuttle craft. The commander manually switched on the shuttle's internal battery power and the navigation computer, but it was unable to perform any command function. The docking arms were locked closed and could not be disengaged. In desperation, the commander switched on the intercom.

"Dr. Dunn, are you there?" Clarendon spoke and then paused to wait for a reply.

"Jim, come in. What are you doing?" He was now more anxious.

Dr. Dunn switched on the intercom.

"It's rather unsettling to be trapped, isn't it?" the doctor spoke with an emotionless monotone voice.

"Doctor, release the docking arms immediately. That's an order!" the commander shouted.

"Our little play is almost finished. The curtain is about to come down," the doctor muttered as he initiated a burn of the retro engines.

The computer screen immediately flashed up a warning that such action could be dangerous. He overrode the warning and started the burn. An alarm sounded on the bridge, and a large warning appeared on the screen:

"Irreversible stall and orbit decay in 4 minutes."

The computer repeated this over and over while counting down the time remaining every fifteen seconds. Commander Clarendon heard the computer over the intercom and saw the retro burn out of the forward windows. He shouted over the intercom for the doctor, but there was no response. The doctor walked to his cabin. He went to his medical cabinet and dispensed several pills, which he swallowed with water. Dr. Dunn lay down on his bed and was unconscious in a few seconds.

The Harite army had reached the summit of the hills that line the east end of the river valley. They stood side by side, thousands of soldiers in a line that stretched out more than five kilometers. An observant watchman on the eastern wall of Amakine noticed the distant figures of men on the hills. An alarm was sounded that brought an abrupt halt to the celebrations and war preparations within the city.

Officers scrambled through the crowd to get up on the wall to see for themselves.

King Malcor and Queen Lea were out on the balcony yet unaware of the Harite soldiers on the hills. The king looked up and noticed what looked like a bright midday star directly overhead. He pointed it out to Lea thinking it was the commander returning in his war chariot. Lea was puzzled and became apprehensive about what she was seeing. Then everyone's attention was drawn to the bright star directly overhead that was quickly becoming larger and brighter in the daylight sky. In the next instant, it was evident that the star was a large ball of white-hot fire speeding toward the center of Amakine. Lea screamed, and before anyone could take another breath, the fireball hit the city with a boom and earthquake that shook the whole valley and the surrounding hills.

A fiery explosion reached to every outer wall and then went straight up. Everyone and everything within the walls of Amakine was either vaporized or blown to pieces. The gates of the city, which were made of heavy timber, were blown off or burned up. The fire at first was brighter than the sun. But as the pillar of flame rose higher into the sky, the brightness of the great fireball diminished and spread out in a large mushroom formation over the valley. Soon, all that remained of Amakine were the great outer walls of stone.

Dust and smoke continued to rise from the city, creating eerie dark brown clouds that covered the whole region, blocking out much of the daylight. The Harite soldiers saw this as the perfect fulfillment of the prophecy. But even they were stunned by the sudden and complete destruction of the city.

Gabriel, Miram, and most of the Harites making their way through the desert saw the top of the great pillar of fire and smoke rising from the other side of the hills. The people were both humbled and encouraged by what they believed to be the awesome power of their god.

The Harite army descended into the valley more than twenty thousand strong. They completely bypassed the once great city of Amakine and marched on Jeku with all of the towns surrounding it.

But they encountered no resistance from a single Amakite. The gates of the city were thrown open to them. As they marched through the city, many Amakites bowed down to the Harite troops either from fear or as a conquered enemy might do seeking mercy from the adversary who prevailed in battle.

Once the city was secured, the Harites would leave a small garrison in it and then advance to the next city. The process was repeated for the remaining three walled cities, producing the same results. In less than two full days, the entire valley was completely subjugated. The Amakites offered no violent resistance. In return, the Harites displayed no hostility toward them. But it was clear to all that the balance of power had shifted. By the time the army had completed its bloodless conquest, the entire Harite population began to pour into the valley.

Miram and most of the Harites had never seen the river valley and the great walled cities in it. She was particularly taken by the river and the valley itself, which was covered as far as the eye could see with crops and grass and trees, everything that is green and growing. The sight was familiar enough to Gabriel, everything except the burned-out city of Amakine with smoke still rising from within its great stone walls.

CHAPTER 18
GABRIEL'S DIARY

In the six months since the Harites reoccupied their valley home, many changes have taken place. All of the statues and temples of the Amakite gods have been destroyed. This is not to say that the Amakites were forced to worship the Harite god, but Harite law now ruled the land, and as the resettlement process was underway, allowances were made for Amakites that have been displaced.

Some of the Amakites in the valley were persuaded by witnessing extraordinary events that the god of the Harites was more powerful than their gods. But some remained inwardly bitter as many husbands, brothers, and sons who served as soldiers were lost. Still, both Harite and Amakite learned to live and work together, and most of the requirements of Harite civil law applied to all people equally. Some Amakites were even being integrated into the military.

Workmen of both races began the long and arduous task of rebuilding the once great city of Amakine, which had its name changed to Jeharesh. The project began by filling in a giant crater that descended eighteen meters at its deepest point. At one time during this period, Gabriel visited the burned-out remains even while hundreds of workers were grading and removing debris. He found little that was recognizable. But as he looked through the dirt and debris piles, he noticed several chunks of metal ranging in size from two centimeters all the way up to about fifty centimeters in length. The metals that he found were not being forged on Ceti 2. Although his training was not in metallurgy, he did recognize pieces of aluminum, chromium, and steel. There were other very hard alloys that he did not recognize. This confirmed to him what he had suspected and feared.

Gabriel could never tell the Harites or even Miram the whole truth about his companions or his origin. He was becoming known among the Harite ecclesiastical hierarchy as a scribe and a historian. He recorded on scrolls in the Harite language all of the major events and acts of the Harite people from the time that he joined them to the present. He based his chronicle on interviews with eyewitnesses along with his own observations. The book was titled simply *The Return* and was judged by the elders to be worthy of a place next to the sacred scrolls of the Harite people. These scrolls, some centuries old, tell the origins of the Harites, their history, and the history of the entire planet even from the very beginning.

Gabriel also kept a diary on an old-style notepad of paper with an ink pen. Dr. Dunn gave him his because he never used it. Gabriel wanted to keep a record that would last for years, and he did not have access to nor did he trust the electronic notepads. This diary he wrote only in English. His thought was that if a future expedition came to the planet, they might find the diary, whether he was alive or dead, and know the story of the first expedition to Eret, which was the Harite word for their world. He did not use dates on his entries because he had lost track of the Earth date, and the Harites had no formal calendar. Instead, he numbered each entry like a chapter heading but with only a number. His diary began on the day that the expedition first landed on Ceti 2.

The following is entry number 62 of Gabriel's diary:

> It has now been about half a year since the destruction of the city of Amakine, now renamed Jeharesh by the Harites. The rebuilding of that once great city has yet barely begun. But the resettlement has pro-

gressed rapidly. Each clan has been given parcels of land or houses within the cities and towns based on their size and their former habitation in the regions they occupied before the exile. Our family has been given about twenty acres outside the walls of Shekem. It has a small house on it which is adequate for shelter until I can build a larger one.

My wife, Miram, told me that she is pregnant. This will be our first child together and perhaps a historic first. Miram's first son, Yakob, is about nine years old by Earth's reckoning. He has accepted me as his father. I feel all of the love, pride, and frustrations that any father could feel for his son. He is intelligent and restless. I am teaching him to be literate in his own language. He is also learning basic concepts of science and mathematics, as far as my limited expertise in these subjects will carry. But Yakob often becomes bored with sitting and taking instruction. He would much rather go out and play with his friends. Their favorite game is war. I guess most nine-year-old boys throughout the universe have this in common. I have taken on the surname of Miram's clan, which is Ker Kadash. This was done to unite our family and guarantee our children their inheritance.

I have not thought much about my former life lately. Sometimes it feels like it was all a dream. These people are intelligent but simple. They enjoy simple pleasures and have a simple faith. It feels good to be a husband and a father. It feels like home.

In my mind, I cannot help but see my former shipmates; of whom I believe only Sandra Hirata and I are still alive. As I noted in an earlier entry, I saw Sandra when we stayed in Jeku on our way to Shekem. We were happy to see each other, but her usual bright and optimistic demeanor seemed suppressed. I did not feel free to pursue the reasons behind it.

The Harites, in general, are a resourceful, generous, and just people. For many of them, including my wife, their faith in their god is very strong. After all that I have experienced and heard about in my time here, the god of the Harites, whatever it is, cannot be ignored or relegated to mythology. I feel compelled to search on for the answer to this great question. As scientists or explorers, we must always seek out the truth—wherever it may lead us and wherever it may be found.

ABOUT THE AUTHOR

Mark McGunegill was born near Los Angeles and grew up in Southern California. A graduate of Santa Ana College, he has been an independent film maker from a very young age and has written two screenplays, one Science Fiction and one Historical Drama. Seeking a career in the film industry, which never panned out, Mark has been employed in various positions in the Construction Industry including Project Superintendent for a major home builder and an independent contractor. Mark has always had an interest in telling his stories in one way or another. STAR TESTAMENT is his first novel.

He currently lives in Southern California with his wife, Susan and his teenage daughter Ashley.

CPSIA information can be obtained
at www.ICGtesting.com
Printed in the USA
FSOW01n1755101214
3788FS